CHAMPION OF FIRE & ICE

CHAMPION OF FIRE & ICE

CHAMPIONS BOOK ONE

MEGAN DERR

CHAPTER ONE

Davrin was drunk when the soft knock came at the chamber door. He nearly ignored it, for who would be coming to see him at so late an hour that he wanted to see? No one.

Two years ago his best friend Ballior had been coldly murdered by King Rorlen's favorite lackies: Lord Tekker and his perpetual, slimy shadow Sir Grayne. A year and a half ago Davrin had learned of it when he'd returned from a diplomatic journey abroad. A year ago mourning had ended, and the cowardly bastards responsible had been sent abroad to murder more people.

A day ago they'd finally returned, and Davrin had issued a challenge. Even His Majesty could not interfere, not unless he wanted to push the patience of his subjects too far and draw an anger that might be more than he could control. Davrin was not the only one angry about Ballior's death; he was simply the only one stupid enough to demand Tekker pay for it.

He'd neglected to remember that point when he'd issued the challenge. The rules of a challenge dictated they each choose a champion, as nobility could not engage in direct combat themselves. Lord Tekker had of course chosen Sir Grayne, who'd accepted promptly.

No one had been willing to face them, leaving Davrin humiliated and devastated. If in the morning he did not have a champion, he would forfeit, and a second challenge could not be issued. Tekker and Grayne were going to get away with beating a man to death simply because he'd dared to stand against them and the new tax laws causing people so much pain.

King Rorlen had done nothing, happier to have a noisy problem resolved than he was troubled that his goons might finally be getting out of hand.

Davrin had no doubt he would soon be seeing Ballior again.

The knock at the door came again, and it was only the softness of it, so unlike the brisk knocks of servants and soldiers, the imperious knocks of nobles and messengers, that compelled him to finally answer it. Heaving himself to his feet, nearly falling on his face in the process, Davrin shuffled-stumbled his way to the door and pulled it open.

His empty cup slipped from his fingers in surprise as he stared at Cimar. "What brings the Master Archivist to my door at so late an hour?"

"Might I come in to have a brief word, my lord?" Cimar asked.

"Of course." Davrin swallowed and

stepped back, suddenly regretting all the brandy he'd imbibed that evening. He closed the door and walked slowly back to his chair at the table by the fireplace, where a nearly-empty decanter of brandy sat beside a long-neglected supper.

Cimar followed behind him and set Davrin's dropped, forgotten cup on the table before taking the seat opposite.

When they'd been much younger, little more than fresh-faced boys thrust too soon into the world of adults, Davrin had dreamed of seeing Cimar in his room. In his bed. In so many situations, some sweet, some hot, many both.

But Cimar had been promised to another, and Davrin had spent much of his life traveling from one troubled spot to another, honing and using his knack for soothing ruffled feathers. Now that he was finally home for a time, taking a well-earned and longer overdue break—unpleasant though it was with justice his only goal now—old feelings he'd thought long faded and gone were proving to have only been quietly slumbering.

Fifteen years had only made Cimar more beautiful, time firming up the youthful roundness of his face, adding sharp edges that Davrin wanted to trace with his fingers before drawing Cimar into a soft kiss. They shared the same light brown skin of the northern part of the country, but where Davrin's hair was dark brown, a heavy mass he kept long as custom dictated, Cimar's was a pale, almost silvery shade that he kept shockingly short, so it feathered about his head in delicate wisps. Currently he was dressed, not in the usual dark blue robes of his office, but black hose and a dark green tunic that brought out the green in his hazel eyes.

"So what can I do for you, Master Archivist?"

"Cimar will suffice," Cimar said softly. "I was away visiting my sister today, or I would have been present for supper, and I regret sorely I was not present."

Davrin's brow furrowed. "Why is that?"

"I would have volunteered to be your champion."

Davrin was grateful he'd not poured himself more brandy. "What? How?"

Cimar laughed, though there was a sour note to the sound. He gestured to the brandy and a second, unused glass next to it. At Davrin's nod, he poured a small measure and took a couple of sips. "Many forget, because I am far more interested in other matters, that I am a knight. I earned my spurs with honor and distinction, and I take the tests every year to keep myself sharp. I know I am not what anyone imagines, but if you still have need of a champion, I would be honored to serve." He drained the brandy in his glass and added softly, "Ballior was my friend, but as a knight I'm forbidden from acting on my own in such fashion. I can only fight on behalf of another."

"I..." Davrin gaped, swallowed, fought an urge to pour more brandy for himself. Tears stung his eyes as he folded his arms on the table and bowed his head. The tears fell to splash on his skin as he said, "The honor would be mine. It is not a debt I could ever repay, asking you to risk your life and health in the name of our dead friend. You know Grayne is a hellhound, yes?" He forced his eyes up, and almost looked away again at the intensity in Cimar's eyes.

Reaching up, Cimar touched the heavy leather collar around his throat that marked him a shifter, one of those rare humans who could turn into a beast. The collar was made of white leather, with a faint silver sheen, and decorated with pearls. What Cimar shifted into, no one knew. Once upon a time it had been law to register such things, but Queen Manna, King Rorlen's grandmother, had changed the law, maintaining that shifters had the right to privacy, especially since they were all too often judged with prejudice on their shifted form.

"I can handle him." Cimar smiled, that sour note returning. "I may be small of frame, but I promise I earned my spurs."

Davrin shook his head. "I do not doubt you. I am sorry I did not realize you were a knight. We met when you were already a scholar in the archives, that's my only feeble excuse. If you are willing to be my champion, then I would have you gladly."

"Then you have me," Cimar said. "I will see you in the field at first bell, my lord."

He stood, and Davrin stood with him, shock and disbelief and cautious hope driving the clouds of alcohol from his brain. He walked Cimar to the door and reached out at the last moment to take his hand and lift it to his lips. "Thank you."

Cimar smiled, and Davrin's breath stopped as he leaned in and up to brush the barest kiss to Davrin's cheek. "Goodnight, my lord."

Then he was gone, leaving only the scent of parchment and ink and beeswax in his wake.

~~*

The rain was still there in the morning, an icy drizzle that foretold a miserable winter. Davrin shivered as he hastened to build up the fire before going to his wardrobe to pull out suitable clothes. Winter hose and shirt, and a tunic in vibrant sky blue—not quite Ballior's house color, but very close to it. Overall he settled his winter cloak, dark forest green wool lined in black fur and trimmed with gray fur. He secured it with a broach Ballior had given him: a gold dragon coiled around the great oak that was Davrin's personal crest.

He coiled his hair into a simple knot, too tired to do more with it right then. The most effort he could muster was a gold, bejeweled hairpin. That done, he pulled on his boots, which were lined with fur as well, keeping him warm as he left the relative warmth of the keep and strode across the yard and out the gates, lifting a hand in greeting to the guards.

Across the bridge and a short distance down the road was the tournament field, where every couple of years the royal family hosted a week-long festival and tournament. Ballior had loved to participate—for the challenge, the reward, the attention. He'd had no interest in love, but plenty of interest in sex, and found no lack of like-minded people at such affairs. The only thing that had ever held Ballior back was money, and that Davrin had more of than he would ever need. He'd been more than happy to have Ballior as his champion and dearest friend.

King Rorlen waited, his toady lord at his side, as well as Crown Princess Korena. She was nothing at all like her loathsome father, much to King Rorlen's vexation—but his wife had died of illness three years ago, and so far he had not married again, so Princess Korena remained his heir. Rumor had it he was going to marry her to Tekker.

If Tekker's standing and reputation survived the challenge and they were indeed married, Davrin hoped she slipped him poison.

Thinking of Tekker not surviving the challenge reminded him that it was all too possible Cimar might *not* survive it. Not that he doubted Cimar's abilities, even if he'd never seen

Cimar as a knight. He feared what sort of underhanded tricks Grayne would employ.

Cimar had said he could handle Grayne, however, and so Davrin would trust him to do so.

Though he could not help the niggle of worry as he reached the tournament field, only to see that his champion had not yet arrived.

King Rorlen looked relieved to see Davrin arrive alone. Tekker sneered, smugness coming off him the way steam wafted off fresh droppings in winter.

When Davrin reached them, King Rorlen shifted restlessly on his horse and said, "I see you're still lacking a champion, Lord Dweller-by-the-Sea."

"Pardon, Your Majesty, but I lack no such thing. My champion is on his way."

"Well, he'd better hurry, or this challenge ends in a forfeit," King Rorlen snapped.

Princess Korena cast her father a brief look but said nothing, only peered down the road. "I believe I see someone coming."

"No one I recognize," Tekker said. "You cannot simply bribe any soldier to be your champion, Davrin."

"I know the law," Davrin said coldly, "and unlike you, I obey it."

"You—" King Rorlen broke off as the figure reached them.

Davrin swallowed. Hard.

Cimar made a beautiful knight, dressed in

the finest plate and a surcoat of black and green, the front emblazoned with a silver rowan tree. His horse was a fine courser, black as ink and more comfortable in the abysmal weather than Grayne's nervous destrier.

He was also making Grayne look a poor show, given Grayne had not bothered to don armor nor even a surcoat, and wore instead clothes better suited to a training field.

Grayne, for the first time, did not look quite his cocky self. Beside him, Tekker's mouth flattened. "Sir Cimar."

"Lord Tekker," Cimar greeted, and dismounted smoothly as he reached Davrin's side. He knelt on the cold ground, one hand splayed for balance, the other across his breast. "Your Majesty, I answer as champion for Lord Davrin Dweller-by-the-Sea in the challenge against Lord Tekker Maldon."

King Rorlen looked as though someone had served him bad meat. "So acknowledged, Sir Cimar. It's been so long since I've seen you away from your dusty shelves, I had forgotten you had the right to wear spurs."

"Many do," Cimar replied.

Princess Korena leaned forward in her saddle. "What compelled you to rise as champion?"

"Lord Ballior was a treasured colleague, and I have always held Lord Davrin in highest esteem."

Tekker sneered. "More like your wife left you and took all the money with her, and we all know Davrin is an easy, desperate mark."

"That is enough," Princess Korena said, voice cracking out like breaking ice. "You will apologize at once."

King Rorlen said nothing, looking out across the field as though not part of the conversation. Fury filled Tekker's face for a bare moment, then he banked it and said, "I owe no apologies to a man who has publicly challenged and humiliated me. I speak only facts, anyway."

Korena stared coldly.

"I'll apologize for speaking the truth if he defeats me in the challenge," Tekker said.

"I appreciate your defense, Your Highness," Davrin said, "but do not trouble yourself. I've heard much the same from him and others of his sort a thousand times. His words don't bother me; they lost that power a long time ago."

"Aye," Cimar agreed. "It would be little better than being offended by the words of a child."

Tekker bristled with renewed rage, but finally King Rorlen dragged himself into the matter and stilled Tekker with a look. "The requirements of the challenge have been met. Now we've to decide what the challenge will be and to set the date. I want this matter concluded before winter's end."

"Say the frost festival," Korena said. "That seems a propitious time to hold a challenge, and this matter has already garnered enough attention, may as well make it a proper spectacle."

Davrin said, "I want the traditional five tests. Greatest number of points wins."

King Rorlen grimaced. "Five would take too long."

"I do not see why it should be more than one, and best of, not points," Tekker said.

"If this is going to be a public affair," King Rorlen said, "then it should be done properly. Five is too many, but I'll grant three. I also agree to the points system, rather than best of. Lord Davrin, did you have tests in mind?"

Davrin wished he'd thought to speak with Cimar ahead of time on the matter, but he'd been so drunk and astonished last night that the details of the matter had escaped him. "Yes, Your Majesty."

"List them. Tekker will have the right to reject one, and I'll pick the final three from there."

That wasn't how it was meant to be done, but Davrin tamped down his frustration and only said, "The tests I had in mind were: Endurance, Quest, Race, Duel, and Joust." He'd picked them with care. Grayne would not be able to resist an endurance challenge or the duel. But he was, for a knight, a terrible horseman and would hate the race and joust, but he'd also hate the quest. Traditionally, the person challenged had the right to discard one test and replace it with his own, but even if he replaced it with one of the easier ones, that left Grayne to face two tests where he was weak. Even with King Rorlen's alteration of the rules, he was left with one guaranteed weakness.

Tekker was a bastard, but he wasn't a fool, and the look on his face said he saw the trap and hated it.

"Lord Tekker, which would you discard?"

Tekker glanced briefly at Grayne, who after a long, strained moment jerked his head. Looking back to King Rorlen, Tekker said, "We discard the race, Your Majesty."

"Very well. I'm discarding the joust. That means, knights, that you will face a quest, a test of endurance, and a duel. I will announce the quests tonight at supper, and you'll have until the opening ceremony of the frost fair to complete them."

"Yes, Your Majesty," the knights chorused.

"Dismissed." He walked off while they were all still bowing and replying.

Korena cast Davrin a bare look, a whisper of a smile on her lips as she nodded in farewell. *Good luck* as plainly as she was allowed to say it.

Tekker and Grayne departed without looking at them, though Davrin had every faith if they could have committed murder right then, they would have. If they'd shown restraint with Ballior, none of them would be here.

When they were gone from sight, and

Davrin and Cimar were alone, Davrin said, "Thank you again for taking up arms for me. I will never forget you did this for me."

Cimar smiled. "The honor is mine. You chose some fine tests. I think Grayne soiled himself when you listed the race and joust. He might have wished for one of those two, however, because the quest is always the most difficult."

"I hope I did not pick any of your weaknesses," Davrin said with a faint smile. "I cannot imagine you have any."

"Endurance could be, depending on the exact nature of it, but I suspect, given the season, that it will be a matter of standing out in the cold in nothing but what the Goddess gave us."

Davrin laughed. "I sort of hope that's true, because Grayne will hate it, but I also do not want you to suffer so." There was also that Cimar was smaller than Grayne, likely to grow cold much faster, but Davrin would not return Cimar's noble gesture by failing to trust him.

"Unlike Grayne, I grew up in this weather." Cimar turned his horse. "Would you like a ride back to the castle, my lord? Why did you walk all this way?"

"I avoid horses as much as possible. They don't like me, and I don't like them. One broken leg was more than enough. Have you had breakfast?" When Cimar shook his head, Davrin said, "I'd be honored if you'd join me in my chambers for a meal, then."

"I am happy to accept that offer." Cimar held out a hand. "Now get on the horse, my lord. I promise you'll come to no harm. I'm an excellent knight, and Frostbite is a fine horse."

Davrin grimaced but took Cimar's hand and clambered up behind him, settling stiffly as they rode off.

"Relax, my lord, and the ride will be much more comfortable."

"If you say so." Davrin rested his head against Cimar's shoulder to ward off the wind biting his face.

But he had to admit it was nice to be back in the castle in only a few minutes rather than the half hour it had taken him to reach the field. Dismounting in the yard, he bowed slightly. "I will arrange breakfast and see you shortly."

Cimar smiled and nodded before riding off to the stables. Davrin turned on his heel and climbed the stairs into the keep.

He flagged down a servant and secured breakfast, then headed off to his rooms. There, he stripped off his gloves and set them aside, then strode over to the fire and warmed himself.

Dozens of thoughts, fears, and doubts rattled around in his head, each one vying for his attention. But it was ultimately the most selfish and frivolous of them that he finally latched onto: was it true that Cimar's wife had left him?

Davrin shouldn't be happy about that, but he'd never thought Mistress Farra a good fit for

Cimar. She was his antithesis, and rare was the instance where combining to such strong opposites made either anything but miserable.

Going to his dressing table, Davrin picked up a comb and set to work on his hair. He worked hard to follow the Goddess's Virtues, but he admitted he faltered slightly when it came to his hair, of which he was proud—even vain. Traditionally, all nobles kept their hair long, as both sign of their station and reminder of their place. Sadly, most nobles remembered the former but forgot the latter. They were too busy being wealthy and powerful to remember to be humble guardians of those entrusted to their care.

When he'd woven it into six braids, he wove those together into a knot at the base of his skull, securing it with a hairpin that was decorated with a white rose at the top—the flower of mourning.

He looked at his reflection and sighed, hands falling to his sides. If only Ballior were still alive, and Cimar was visiting his chambers for an entirely different reason. No matter how impossible it was, and even with all the years that had passed, Davrin still pined for the impossible. But maybe… maybe when all of this was over… he could see what might be possible.

Romantic and sexual relationships between lords and knights were not forbidden, but they were generally frowned upon, given their respective stations and duties. The laws that governed the lords and ladies of the kingdom were:

> *To Respect the Goddess and Keep Her Temple*
> *To Serve the Crown Faithfully and Diligently*
> *To Care for the People and Maintain the Kingdom*
> *To Speak for the Welfare of All*
> *To Succor the Weak and Abandoned*
> *To Be Honest, Diligent, and Kind*
> *To Do No Harm*
> *To Never by Dishonorable Means Cause Harm to be Done*
> *To Refuse No Challenges Brought by an Equal*
> *To Live Nobly and Wisely*

Knights, meant to serve, had their own list of strictures to live by:

> *To Respect the Goddess and Fight in Her Name*
> *To Defend the Crown at All Costs*
> *To Protect the People and Guard the Kingdom*
> *To Fight for the Welfare of All*
> *To Rescue the Weak and Abandoned*
> *To Be Courageous, Steadfast, and Merciful*
> *To Bring Harm Only as a Last Recourse*
> *To Never by Dishonorable Means Harm or Cause Harm to be Done*
> *To Answer as Champion when Called Upon*
> *To Live Honorably and Humbly*

They were meant always to work in tandem, nobles and knights, but never intimately. A noble too close to a knight relied over much on the sword to solve his problems; a knight too close to a noble found his edge dulled; both found themselves less earnest in their duties.

And, naturally, the crown preferred to keep its different powers clearly divided and more easily controlled. So marriage was forbidden, intimate relationships strongly discouraged, and even friendships should not run too deep.

Of course, all of that was overlooked by His Majesty when it came to Lord Tekker and Sir Grayne, who were like fire and a parched forest. Those two were every reason nobles and knights were expected to maintain a certain distance, but why should King Rorlen care?

Leaving the bedroom, he went to the front room, where breakfast had been arranged on the table. He'd just poured ale for himself and Cimar when a knock came at his door.

He opened it and bowed slightly as he stepped back to let Cimar into the room.

Cimar had traded his armor for his more familiar hose and long tunic, though he'd retained his heavy cloak against the cold, drafty castle. It was blue, trimmed and lined in silvery-white fur that almost perfectly matched his hair, making him look like some sprite sent to mete out justice—or mischief—on behalf of the Goddess herself.

"That breakfast looks delicious," Cimar said.

Normally breakfast was a lowkey affair, usually just gruel and hot ale before setting to work for the day. Even in the royal castle, there was rarely more than that. Growing up, Davrin hadn't thought anything of it. He ate his gruel, set to work, and stopped like everyone else at midday for the main meal.

But years of schooling, where a big breakfast was served and midmeal was small, if not skipped or missed entirely due to classes, had changed his habits. Living abroad had only separated him further from the practice, and even now that he was home, he preferred a strong meal at the start of the day, no matter the odd looks it gained him.

"It does," he agreed, and passed over a cup of hot ale before settling into his seat with his own cup. He sipped the ale, which was heavily spiced and fruity, then set about smearing pieces of bread with butter and honey, filling a bowl of porridge with nuts, dried fruit, and cheese. "Thank you again for helping me. I will never be able to repay you."

"There is nothing to repay, my lord." Cimar took a sip of ale. "As I said before, Ballior was my friend too. That aside, I am a knight, and it is my duty and honor to serve those in need. I may spend my days with books, but they were not the reason I became a knight. They're simply where I've always proven to be most useful."

Davrin stuffed his mouth with cheese to prevent injudicious words slipping out. Now was not the time. "So what do you think our esteemed monarch will choose for the quests?"

Cimar grimaced and traced the rim of his cup as he replied, "I'm afraid to think about it, frankly. The frost festival is just weeks away, so that restricts what he *can* choose—and the weather limits it even further." He snorted. "He will certainly give Grayne something easy, and me something difficult."

Rolling his eyes, Davrin refilled both their cups, then settled back in his seat. "His Majesty prefers to combine problems where he can, so I suspect you will be sent to deal with the bandits in the mountain. I know the problem has finally gotten bad enough he was getting ready to send out royal troops to deal with it. Cheaper to send you, and either get a lot of dead bandits or a canceled challenge."

"Oh, Goddess, I think you're right." Cimar groaned, drained his ale, and set the cup down with a hard clack on the table. "I suppose at least we will be rid of those damned bandits."

Davrin's shoulders tightened. "Just do not get yourself killed. I want justice for Ballior, but not at the cost of your life. Of anyone's life." His shoulders slumped. "Perhaps this was selfish of me. I—"

"You are doing what the law requires, and right by your oldest and dearest friend. I am a knight, trust that I know what that entails and that I made my choice."

Bowing his head slightly, Davrin replied, "Of course, my apologies. I intended no disrespect. I'm sorry I gave it."

Cimar lifted a hand. "Not at all. I'm honored you'd worry so over me, my lord."

"I think you can leave off the formalities, at least when it's only the two of us. Please, Davrin is fine."

"As you wish. So quest is likely to be bandits, the endurance I feel will be seeing who can last the longest in the freezing cold, which leaves only the duel."

"He's going to cheat," Davrin said.

Cimar snorted and shrugged. "I admit I'm not looking forward to it, but I can handle him."

"I never doubted that. Now, enough grim talk. Enjoy your food. Will you be going to the archives for the rest of the day?"

"No, I need to finish readying the rest of my equipment and run my horses through their paces. If I am going questing, I'll need my palfrey and rouncey ready. They've not done much but run me through fields the past few months, though I always try to make sure it's good exercise, not merely token." He chuckled softly. "I will also need to drag my errant squire out of whatever tavern he's fallen asleep in."

Davrin quirked a brow. "You have a squire? Who's.. a drunkard?"

"Drunkard, no. He simply likes to have fun and end his nights with anyone willing and eager." Cimar smiled. "He's a bit of a brat, but he's got a good heart and works hard. So I let him go off to play when he can. We were scheduled to escort a shipment of books from Golden Apple Abbey next week. It would have been a brutal journey."

Wincing, Davrin replied, "Yes, that road is more bandit than paving stone. I didn't realize you went on those journeys as the armed guard."

Cimar's mouth quirked in a mischievous little grin. "Like I've said before, everyone forgets I'm a knight, and I make no production of it, because I do believe in the credo that ours is to serve, not to grandstand."

"You do yourself, your spurs, and your fellows proud," Davrin said softly. "Ballior would be humbled to have you fight in his honor."

Cimar rose and bowed slightly. "The honor is mine." He started to leave, then stilled and turned back. "There was one more thing, my lord—I mean, Davrin."

Davrin stood as well and moved slightly closer to him. "What's that?"

"What they said about my wife and needing money." Cimar's mouth flattened. "I'm not doing this for money. I don't *need* money, whatever rumors are floating around the castle.

Rosa didn't leave me; we parted on good terms, as friends. She desperately wanted children, and between the two of us, we could never manage it. So we parted, and she's found a fine farmer. They're quite happy together. I visit them every couple of months. We've never been able to legally end our marriage, since we must have His Majesty's permission for that, and he won't grant it, but we've all done the best we can."

"I'm glad." Davrin gripped his shoulder briefly. "You owed me no explanations, and your integrity was never in doubt."

Cimar replied with a fleeting smile, then bowed again before departing, the door closing quietly behind him.

Davrin sighed, scrubbed his face to banish all the bothersome *feelings* drive him to insanity, and went to go tackle more of the mountain-high pile of correspondence that had been awaiting his arrival.

CHAPTER TWO

It took Cimar an hour to find his squire, and most of that was walking into and through town and being forced to stop and chat with people.

Thankfully, Leonine was right where Cimar had expected to find him: at the Golden Rooster (called the Gold Cock by locals), in the innkeeper's bed, snoring softly where he was cuddled between the innkeeper and his wife.

Cimar rolled his eyes, but a smile twitched at his mouth. He stepped close to the bed and shook Leonine's foot.

Groaning, Leonine cracked an eye open. "Hmm?"

"Come on, Lee. There's a quest to prepare for."

Leonine's eyes popped wide at that, and he dropped quick kisses on the mouths of his slowly-stirring companions before crawling out of bed.

Cimar went to wait in the bar while he dressed and said his goodbyes.

Several minutes later, Lee came out dressed but somehow *more* mussed.

"Got a goodbye kiss, did we?"

Lee grinned. "Goodbye something."

Cimar lifted his eyes to the ceiling and cuffed him playfully. "Come along, dear squire."

"So what is this about a quest?" Lee asked, pausing to buy a meat pie from a vendor before they threaded back through town toward the castle.

By the time Cimar finished explaining everything, Lee was laughing between bites of his pie. "Of course, this is only about Ballior. Not at all about the fact—"

"Let's discuss your romance, shall we? I notice you spend more time at the Gold Cock than anywhere else, and when you go other places, it's only to drink and play games, not to fuck. What's that about?"

Lee made a face. "All right, all right. I'll stop teasing you about your infatuation with Lord Dweller-by-the-Sea."

Cimar stopped, catching Lee's arm to make him do the same. "Are you all right?"

"I'm fine," Lee said, though his smile was heavy.

"Are they treating you poorly?"

"No, they're looking for fun, and I'm happy to provide it."

Cimar sighed, let him go, and resumed walking. "I see. If you need anything—"

"I know. You've always been there for me, and I appreciate it. So is Lord Dweller happy to have you as his champion?"

"As happy as one can be, given the circumstances, I suppose." Cimar shrugged one shoulder. "The man is a highly skilled diplomat. He gives away only those thoughts and emotions he intends. Now enough gossiping. Ready the horses. We're going to run them through their paces a few times. I pulled out Frostbite this morning, but the others need attending. My plate is fine, and my spare chain, but—"

Lee cut him off with a snorting laugh. "I know what needs to be done better than you!"

Cimar smiled. "Then get to work, knave."

With an elaborate court bow that had Cimar shoving him, Lee laughed and ran off.

Cimar followed more sedately, heading around the keep as he reached it and straight for the temple and the enormous building connected to it by a beautiful hallway of glass and wood— the royal library and archives.

Thankfully, unknown to most, he'd already begun withdrawing from his duties as Master Archivist. The job had grown entirely too political and easy for his taste. He might not be a lad anymore, but he had enough life left in him to want something different. Archivist had suited him once; now he wanted something different.

Something that involved Davrin, if he stood even the slightest chance of making that happen, and stupid, pointless laws be damned. If Sir Grayne could flout every single line of the code, Cimar could ignore the admonitions against intimate relations with a noble.

Once he'd checked in with Theodora that all was well and nothing required his attention, he returned to his rooms to set to work on his clothing. It had been a long time since he'd needed any of his knightly finery. Normally he just wore the robes of the librarians, with a patch to mark his rank and cords to mark his specialties.

The rowan tree surcoat he'd worn earlier that morning was still on the bed where he'd set it. His armor and weapons were all gone, carted off by Leo to be repaired, cleaned, and whatever else Leo decided was required.

Going to one of his clothing trunks, Cimar pulled out his other surcoats, his leathers, and his sewing and repair kits.

The leathers he'd leave for Leo; he was much better at that. The surcoats Cimar would tend to himself. He'd always had a deft hand for sewing and liked the work besides. The youngest of seven boys, his mother had needed someone to help her, and there'd been no daughters or nieces or fosters. So Cimar it had been, and whatever teasing he sometimes got for doing women's work, he'd always vastly preferred it to being in the fields all day. It had also given him an opportunity to learn his letters and more. Without his mother's sewing, he'd probably still be a farm boy.

So he would always be happy to stitch and

repair his own clothes.

He hummed some of his favorite hymns as he smoothed out his white tunic. The embroidery along the edges was faded and torn in several places. It took him the rest of the morning and well into the afternoon to cut everything away and pin the new hems.

When he finally made himself stop, it was only because his eyes were sore, and his stomach was on the verge of staging a rebellion.

He slipped down to the kitchen and absconded with a bowl of stew, a plate of additional victuals, and a pitcher of beer before the head cook could catch him, winking at the scullery maids who *did* spy him, grinning when they muffled giggles and snickers with the backs of their soapy hands.

Back up in his room, it was to find Lee had returned, freshly cleaned and already setting to work on repairing the leathers. "How are my beasts?"

"As bratty as ever," Lee said cheerfully. "I think they know they're finally going to be put to some hard use and are eagerly awaiting it. The castle is positively beside itself with excitement over the latest gossip. Everyone is placing bets, and there's all sorts of theories about why you've stepped forward as champion, everything from you're desperate for money to secretly Lord Dweller's lover."

"Well, that's just the typical sort of rumors.

Nothing creative at all?"

"It is only the first day."

"Mm, true enough. Come and eat, Lee, then we'll get back to work for a bit, though it's so dark now, I'm not sure we can work for much longer, even with the fire and these lamps."

They settled at the small square table shoved into one corner of the room, which Lee diligently kept tidy despite Cimar's perpetual attempts to keep it cluttered. Lee poured the beer, and they dug into the meal with gusto. That afternoon's dinner was a hearty venison stew, the gravy thick, the vegetables and meat plentiful, and the seasoning generous. No one ever left King Rorlen's table complaining of the food, that was for certain.

After a lifetime spent eating little more than vegetables and the occasional poached rabbit, Cimar was eternally grateful for the veritable feasts he now got to consume nightly, to say nothing of breakfast and the actual feast that would be supper later that night.

"Do your lovers know you'll be gone for a time, questing and then attending me the rest of the challenge? I would hate for them to think you've strayed to newer pastures."

Lee smiled faintly. "Came to see me at the castle, they did, and said they'd come and cheer for you if they could find the time."

"Oh, ho, methinks they're not just after a touch of fun after all. Or as usual, you're just too pretty to be ignored."

That got him a laugh and a cautiously happy, hopeful look that he hoped did not prove in vain. Lee deserved someone—or two someones—who would appreciate him as he was. Too many marked him a knave and a slut, and discounted him out of hand. But Lee was a fine man, a fine squire, and someday would be an excellent knight. Soon, in fact. Once this challenge was completed… even if Cimar lost, it would be more than enough to prove Lee's training had gone as far as Cimar could take him.

One thing at a time. He took a deep swallow of beer and returned to his food.

Lee grinned. "It's not *my* prettiness the castle is talking about. Everyone has something to say about how fine a knight you look all gilded up. They're all starting to wonder who the real problem in your marriage is if that's how you look when you're not in your 'dull, stodgy, bookish robes.'"

"I see." Cimar didn't roll his eyes, but it was a near thing.

Lee, never one to miss the slightest detail, grinned slyly. "The real question is, does Lord Dweller like the way you look in your armor? How interested is he in seeing you out of it?"

"Enough. Bottle that energy you're wasting on teasing me and put it to use on getting my leathers back in shape."

"Oh, please, like they even need that much

work. The only reasons you have so much sewing to do is that you wear the same two tunics all the time and those ugly robes, so the stuff that actually looks good on you has been left to languish."

"Enough," Cimar repeated. "Or I'll find plenty of work to keep you too busy to run your mouth."

Lee rolled his eyes but mercifully fell silent and focused on his meal, leaving Cimar once more to his thoughts.

Though he'd tried not to show it in front of Davrin, the quest had him concerned. He definitely thought the bandits were a likely possibility, but it seemed far more likely that was the easy quest that would go to Grayne.

"What other rumors have you heard?" he asked. "Along the lines of those bandits to the north."

Lee frowned, tapping his spoon against the rim of the large bowl they shared. "There's some trouble in town, though I don't know that's reached the castle yet. Some particularly nasty brigands have been accosting travelers and locals alike, leaving them severely injured and minus their valuables. Rumor has it a few people have been killed, but I can't find anything to confirm that. Everyone is being too cagey. Makes me think they know who's responsible, and nobody wants to be the one who gets a red necklace for opening their mouth. The usual river pirates, of course, and whispers that our latest book-fetching trip will bring more trouble than usual." He pursed his lips. "Some chatter about blackmail in the castle, did you want that?"

At that, Cimar did rolls his eyes. "If I asked you to detail to me the latest list of blackmailings about the castle, we'd be here until the next full moon. No, I think you've given me what I need." He gnawed at his bottom lip as his thoughts turned and turned.

Very nearly the only true advantage he had was that no one knew what kind of shifter he was, which meant King Rorlen and his pair of cronies could not use it against him. They couldn't factor it in at all. He'd always been deeply protective and private of his shifted form. Only Rosa, Leonine, and his mentor knew what shape he took. No one else. Cimar preferred to keep it that way, but above and beyond all else, he wanted to help Davrin and obtain justice for Ballior.

"What are you going to wear tonight?" Lee asked.

"Something…how did you say it earlier? Gilded. Grayne may not take his position, or this situation, seriously, but I do, and I want the whole court to note the difference."

Lee grinned, slow and mischievous and just one of the many reasons Cimar was proud and delighted to have him for a squire. Finishing his food, he arranged the dirty dishes neatly on the tray and rose. "I'll take all this back to the kitchen, then get your supper clothes ready before resuming work on the leathers. I won't have everything done, but I'll get enough of it, and the rest I can finish while we travel."

"Sounds a fine plan." Lee departed, and Cimar returned to his sewing, finishing up the hems easily enough and moving on to start on new embroidery. That would take him an age, even as simple as it was, but there was nothing to be done about that.

Many knights didn't even bother, considering such frivolities beneath them. The reality was that those who didn't have women they could make do the work would rather spend the money on beer and the like than on clothes they'd just ruin in a fight anyway. For most of them, clothes were something to be easily replaced. They'd never known what it was like to make clothes from whatever scraps they could find, with embroidery and other needlework the only way to make it remotely pretty.

He hummed softly as he started on the tunic he'd wear when he returned from the quest. It was a deep midnight blue, with his rowan tree crest in delicate gray. Before, he'd embroidered the hem in a simple leaves and flowers design. This time, though, he rather favored stars, with larger ones in gray thread and smaller ones in soft amber that was closer to gold. It would take longer, but be worth the effort.

After this one, he'd tackle his emerald

green tunic, though what design he'd use for that, he had no idea. But it was his finest one, and he would wear it when he won the challenge. There was no other outcome he would tolerate. The only way he'd accept loss was if Grayne killed him, which Grayne would likely try to do at least once, but Cimar would be damned if he lost to that worthless excuse of a knight, especially over the matter of a fallen comrade's honor, *especially* when he was fighting on behalf of Davrin.

Cimar took a deep breath and paid more care to his stitches as he realized he was yanking at the thread. He focused on happier thoughts as he worked: of Davrin, of getting to travel about for a short time, even if it were to roust bandits. Spending time with Lee, his horses, getting to put the skills he'd worked so hard on to real use.

Lee returned several minutes later, looking pleased with himself, so some sort of mischief had been accomplished. Humming along with Cimar, he set immediately to work preparing his clothes for that evening, a beautiful ice blue tunic with a geometric diamond pattern that had taken Cimar months of work, his perpetual rowan meticulously stitched so the diamond pattern spread out from it, leaving the tree itself hollow, noticeable for the absence of the pattern that was everywhere else. There were matching hose and shoes to go with it, but thankfully none of the elaborate nonsense for his hair that was so popular at the moment, as he kept his short and safely away from the labors and headaches of courtly fashion.

"Do you want the white cloak or the gray with this?"

"White."

Lee nodded and went back to work, and so far as Cimar's days went, it was one of the most pleasant he'd enjoyed in a long time.

~~*

Some hours later, bathed and dressed and fussed over by Lee, despite the fact he was perfectly capable of dressing himself, Cimar said, "Thank you, Lee. You're welcome to join me if you like, as ever, but by all means go spend the night with your lovers. Just be back here before dawn, since the earlier we head out, the better, and I can't imagine His Majesty will give us anything that doesn't send us miles upon miles away."

"I will. Thank you, my lord. Now get."

Cimar left the peace and quiet of his room and headed off to the contained chaos of the dining hall, where no doubt it would be far more crowded than usual as everyone came to see for themselves what the quest would be, and if it really was Cimar who'd answered as champion for Lord Davrin Dweller-by-the-Sea.

He hated to be the center of attention. It was one of the reasons he'd always been perfectly content to while his days away in the archives, leaving only to make the arduous journey to see new books and other contributions arrived safely. There was no help for it, though. Davrin was a highly respected figure at court and abroad, which made him powerful—not so powerful anyone else had been willing to tangle directly with Lord Tekker, but now that the fight was on, they would likely lend whatever quiet support they could.

If—when—Cimar won, they would be more than happy to throw their lot in with ensuring Tekker stayed toppled. King's favorite thug he might be, Tekker was almost universally hated by everyone else, including Her Royal Highness. The moment he showed a weakness they could exploit, that would be the end of Tekker and his nasty little hellhound Grayne.

One of the heralds announced his arrival, and the room fell silent as he entered. That was a first. Hopefully a last, but given the fun had not yet even begun, likely that hope was in vain.

Steeling himself, head up, shoulders high, well-honed calm in place, Cimar strode evenly through the hall until he was before the High Table. He knelt, one hand splayed, the other across his breast. "Your Majesty. Your Highness. I bid you good evening."

"Rise, Sir Cimar. Join your lord."

"Majesty." Cimar rose and then bowed to Davrin, who smiled and motioned for him to take a chair. Surprisingly, Davrin was seated to the left of Princess Korena, when normally Cimar would have sworn he sat opposite and a few chairs down. Korena must be up to something.

Not certain he wanted to know what, but equally certain he'd find out anyway, Cimar took his seat and beckoned a servant to bring him wine. Thankfully, his location put him well away from Tekker and Grayne.

Unsurprisingly, the meal was painfully typical and dragged on forever. Not because His Majesty wanted to build anticipation, but because he was stalling on dealing with a problem for as long as possible.

Finally, though, as the bells rang the ninth hour, His Majesty rose and said, "Lords, Knights of the Challenge, assemble before me."

Cimar rose and followed Davrin around the table, down the steps of the dais, to once more kneel before King Rorlen. Close by, Korena's face gave nothing away, but Cimar didn't think he was crazy in thinking she looked well tired of her father's behavior.

"Rise," King Rorlen said, and Cimar rose smoothly alongside the other three. Grayne, predictably, was already well into his cups and nearly fell right back on his face. Cimar didn't sneer openly, but only with great effort.

Standing, King Rorlen threw out his arms to command silence, then said in strident tones, "A challenge has been called and answered. On behalf of our fallen comrade, Sir Ballior Windon,

Knight of the Order of the Star, a challenge has been called by Lord Davrin Dweller-by-the-Sea, Earl of Broken Cliff. Sir Cimar Vallion, Knight of the Order of the Star, has answered as his champion. He challenges Lord Tekker Malden, Marquis of Maldenor, who has accepted. Sir Grayne Darmount, Knight of the Order of Blood, has answered as his champion. These champions will face three challenges: quest, to be called tonight; endurance, to be faced upon the onset of the frost fair; and duel, which will be faced on the final day of the fair."

He spread his arms again. "Is there any who would denounce this challenge as dishonorable or unjust?"

Silence rang out through the enormous hall, and Cimar didn't think he imagined the annoyance—even fury—that flickered ever so briefly across King Rorlen's face.

"Then let the challenge begin, and here knights are your quests:

"Sir Grayne, bandits and brigands have plagued the road to the Golden Apple Abbey for years. Locate the source of the problem and destroy it once and for all, that people might once more travel that road in safety."

"Your Majesty."

Amusement curled through Cimar. So Grayne was being ordered to fix the problem that Cimar supposedly couldn't. Did they think he was going to be insulted by something so childish and petty?

When it was clear no reaction was forthcoming, King Rorlen continued in a sour tone, "Sir Cimar, far to the north is Castle Bone. Its inhabitants have not been heard from in months, and no messenger sent there ever returns. Journey there and resolve the mystery, that we might know what has become of that place."

"Your Majesty." Next to Cimar, Davrin of course gave nothing away, but it wasn't hard to guess that he was furious with the quests: Grayne's simple and close to home, where he could easily cheat and would have all the time in the world for the quest itself while sleeping in his own bed almost every night.

Cimar, meanwhile, would spend most of his quest on arduous travel during the darkest, coldest, most dangerous part of the year. When he reached his destination, he was likely to find one of two things: the castle had been overtaken by some manner of enemy, or it had been wiped out by sickness. Either one posed a great risk to a man expected to face such a challenge with only his squire at his side.

The imbalance was so offensive it was almost laughable. He remained silent, though, as did Davrin, who knew better than most the value and wisdom in silence.

"The quests begin at sunrise. You're dismissed." King Rorlen snapped his fingers, and his attendants and bodyguards enfolded him and follow him from the hall.

Cimar rose, and Davrin beside him. They shared a look, and as one departed the hall in the opposite direction, bound for Davrin's chambers. The door slammed shut behind them, and Davrin's notorious calm façade cracked like a dropped plate. "I have really and truly had it with him."

"At least he's fairly predictable in his vindictiveness," Cimar replied. "I admit neither I nor Leonine thought of Castle Bone, but we should have. It's nothing I haven't deal with before, be it brigands or plague."

Davrin's ire immediately turned into concern. "Brigands concern me far less than plague. Only the Goddess herself can spare a man from that horrid fate. I hope I have not sought justice for Ballior only to lose you too."

"It is your right to call a challenge and my right to answer as champion. Recriminations waste energy and time. Leave off them. You're a diplomat of no small renown; you know all this."

Smiling faintly, Davrin replied, "That is true. I even anticipated His Majesty would act the vindictive child over the matter, but he is surprising even me with how apathetic and mean he's been."

"It's a wonder to me a man like that produced someone as fine and honorable as Princess Korena," Cimar said. "She is on our side, I feel, and that counts for much."

Davrin nodded, brow furrowing briefly as his thoughts took him. Cimar left him to them, taking a seat at the table where they'd had breakfast only hours ago, and focused on his own thoughts.

Such as the best way to reach Castle Bone. It was well into the mountains, high enough up that those unaccustomed to the height struggled to breath at first. Once upon a time it had been a key defense post, but treaties formed nearly two generations ago now had reduced it to little more than a throughway when easier paths were rendered unusable by the mercurial mountains.

Theoretically they could reach it by horse, but that relied heavily on the road and the weather being kind to them, and that the problem was easily resolved or at least deduced in a matter of days, giving them plenty of time to return. He was going to have little choice but to use his shifted form if they wanted any real chance of completing the quest.

Which King Rorlen probably knew. Or at least hoped. Either they went by horse and risked failing, or he used his shifted form and with it thus revealed, bared himself to whatever conniving King Rorlen and his repugnant lackies came up with to exploit it.

Cimar wasn't nearly as stupid as they clearly thought, however.

"I'm glad you seem far less troubled by all of this than me," Davrin said, joining him at the table. "Ballior could have no better champion, truly."

"The honor is mine to stand for a fallen friend. Do not worry about His Majesty's machinations. He vastly underestimates how much conniving is involved in the archives. Trust me, monarchs and nobles have nothing on scribes, monks, and nuns when they are bickering over who gets what manuscripts and who is the best at making new copies of the tomes in their keeping." He smiled faintly. "The last time I was at the Golden Apple, a fist fight broke out, and nobody throws a punch like a vexed abbess."

To his delight, Davrin burst into laughter, the kind of open, delighted laugh he seldom showed, let alone so easily. A victory on the battlefields was not nearly as pleasing as being the reason for that laugh. It took everything Cimar possessed not to openly preen.

"Shall we have a drink?" Davrin asked as his laughter faded, leaving behind a smile that Cimar ached to taste. "Then I will let you be on your way to enjoy a good night's rest, since you have a long, arduous road ahead of you."

"A drink sounds wonderful."

Before Davrin could pour them, however, a brisk, commanding knock came at the door. Frowning slightly, Davrin went to answer it—and stepped back a moment later to admit Lady Aliara, Princess Korena's favored lady-in-waiting. On her right arm she wore a thick leather bracer, on which was perched a beautiful white peregrine.

"Milady," Davrin said, sketching her a bow. Cimar rose and did the same, remaining on his feet when she politely rejected Davrin's offer of a seat.

"I come at the bidding of my princess, to offer you a token for your journey, Sir Cimar."

His eyes widened. "Her Highness is granting me use of one of her peregrines?"

Aliara bowed her head in a graceful nod. "Such tokens are well within the boundaries of a challenge, and Her Highness feels it prudent you have an effective means of communication should you find circumstances are as bad as, or even worse than, expected at Castle Bone." She gave a sharp whistle, and the peregrine flew to one of the chairs and perched on the back of it. Removing the leather bracer, she gave it to Cimar. "If there was time, I'd have one made properly for you, but this one is adjustable and should suffice. Her name is Valor, and if you have the time now, I will teach you the commands you'll need."

"I most definitely have the time for that," Cimar said. "My lord, I regret we must share our drink at another time."

Davrin waved the words away. "The drinks will keep. I bid you both a good night."

Once the bracer was in place on Cimar's arm, Aliara gave another whistle—rather a sharp pair of them—and as Cimar lifted his arm the way she instructed, Valor flew straight to it.

"She's beautiful," Cimar said. "Good night, my lord. I look forward to sharing that drink upon my return."

Davrin bowed his head, and Cimar followed Aliara from the room and through the halls to the courtyard where Princess Korena kept and trained her beloved raptors.

A few hours later, well into midnight, he felt reasonably confident in his abilities to at least ensure Valor made it home with vital information should that be necessary. He dragged himself back to his room to get a precious few hours of sleep before he must rise so he and Lee could be on their way when the sun rose.

Thankfully, Lee returned shortly before he rose, saving him a trip into town. As they packed up a few last-minute items, he explained the details of the quest.

"I'm going to have some choice things to say about His Majesty when we're alone in the woods with no one to hear them," Lee hissed as he finished. "This is flagrant abuse and favoritism! He isn't even trying to be subtle."

"You don't have to be subtle when you're nigh untouchable," Cimar replied dryly. "Come on." He slung his saddlebags over his shoulder and led the way through the castle and across the yard to the enormous royal stables. Lee must have spoken with them at some point, because all four of the horses they'd need for this journey were ready and waiting. Strapping saddlebags in place, Cimar swung into the saddle, pulled up the hood his cloak, and led the way through the portcullis and over the drawbridge, lowered earlier than usual just for him—and presumably Grayne, though Cimar doubted he'd rise any time soon, if he bothered to begin his quest at all that day.

Once they were beyond the walls, he gave three clear, sharp whistles. A moment later, Valor came soaring toward him and landed on his shoulder like she'd done it a thousand times.

"Well, that will make obtaining food a good sight easier."

Cimar laughed. "Of course you go straight to food and not having to do the hunting yourself."

Lee grinned and began to sing as they headed off. Their goal was to reach the foothills by dark and stable the horses at a reputable tavern in the traverse town there. Once dark had well and truly fallen, Cimar would then shift and fly them the rest of the way to Castle Bone, turning a trip of at least two weeks into one of a matter of hours.

He couldn't wait to see Grayne's face when he returned weeks early and with his shifted form still a secret. If they wanted to win via cheating, they were going to have to work a whole lot harder.

CHAPTER THREE

Davrin had hoped a good night's rest would see him soothed, but when he woke shortly after sunrise he was still fuming about the flagrant mistreatment of his champion—of his challenge. He had not called it lightly, no challenge was ever called lightly, and yet His Majesty was treating it like a game, a silly inconvenience he must endure and wanted over as soon as possible. He wasn't even trying to pretend otherwise.

If His Majesty's selfish apathy caused Cimar to die of the plague—to die, period, as a result of such flagrant favoritism and sabotage—Davrin would teach him how foolish it was to betray a courtier who'd been unfailingly loyal his whole life.

Biting back his anger as he had so many times when locked in discussions with stubborn fools where prejudice and cultural differences made everything ten times harder, Davrin threw back the blankets and climbed out of bed, hastening into the heavy wool dressing robe hanging nearby. Then he stoked the fire and got a pot of tea going.

One of the castle servants would be along shortly with breakfast. Normally, he had a personal manservant to manage such things, but Geoff had recently married and returned with his wife to her farm, and Davrin had not yet had time to replace him.

When breakfast came, he set it and his tea on the table near the fire, feet shoved into thick, fur-lined slippers that did a fairly good job of warding off the bitingly cold stone floor.

Normally he would have five hundred things to do—meetings, negotiations, taking visitors about the city, arranging meetings, and more. But with the challenge called, that was his sole focus, as he could not do anything that might be taken, accidentally or otherwise, as currying favor or otherwise cheating.

Which left him with a pile of correspondence to tackle, some financial matters for his estates, and not much else. He wouldn't see Cimar for at least a month, if all went perfectly, and more if something went wrong. Never again if the quest ended in disaster.

Taking a deep breath, he once more turned his thoughts to other matters. Few they were, but anything was better than brooding and steeping in his own ire.

He'd only just settled into a rhythm with his mountain of correspondence when a soft knock came at his door. Standing, Davrin turned—and stared bemused as a sealed slip of paper was slid under his door. What in the world?

Striding across the room, he knelt to retrieve it, frowning at the unmarked blue wax that closed it. Generic, the kind of wax used in temples, where people who couldn't read and write, or afford the supplies, went to have letters and such written for them. The paper was slightly better quality than that, but only just.

Returning to his desk, he picked up the crystal-handled letter opener that had been a gift from Ballior years ago, part of a handsome desk set Davrin still treasured. Slicing the wax seal, he set the opener aside and flipped the letter open. The contents did not lessen his bemusement.

Farlow. Old grotto. Two hours. Knock three times on door to acknowledge receipt.

Who in the world wanted a secret meeting with him, and in such a remote place? It would take nearly all of the two hours to reach it, assuming horse and weather cooperated, which were not assumptions he would lay a single pence on.

Striding back across the room, he rapped three times on his door. An answering knock came and then he heard steps hasten down the hall. Shaking his head, he threw the letter in the fireplace and went to his wardrobe.

Half an hour later, he was heading away from the castle, precious minutes wasted to drop enough word with guards and servants that anyone looking for him would be told he'd gone into the city to run some errands. He'd also paid a girl to run a few errands for him, and to leave the purchases at an inn he'd used before for such matters, so that when he returned home later it would indeed look like he'd spent his day on mundane chores.

He rode as quickly as the horse was comfortable doing, hating every single moment of it. The weather was bitterly cold, the kind of cold so deep that even snow wouldn't fall, and the snow already on the ground crunched and snapped like broken glass. He had the best cloak, the best furs, that money could buy without getting into smuggling and other illicit methods, and still he was cold all the way to his bones.

Hopefully Cimar and his squire were doing all right, because the weather wasn't going to get any kinder the further north they went.

The overcast sky made the journey gloomy, and the lack of any other life along the old road leading to Farlow, or what was left of it anyway, made everything dreary and slightly creepy.

He reached Farlow just past the two hour mark, but hopefully his mysterious host to this strange meeting would forgive him being a few minutes late.

Farlow stretched out before him, derelict and depressing. It had been a happy, bustling little town once, well known for its cider, but plague had wiped out nearly all the residents, and those few who survived had been quarantined in the temple for weeks, until all signs of illness had passed. The victims had been burned and scattered, survivors eventually permitted to leave but allowed to take nothing with them on the chance the disease lingered. They'd been compensated by the crown, but gold didn't replace the heirlooms and memories they'd been forced to leave behind.

Since then, lowlifes of all sorts had stripped the place clean of those treasures, hopefully not taking the plague with them. Six years had passed since, and with each one the surrounding woods reclaimed the abandoned town a little bit more. A few more years and no signs of it would remain.

He pushed onward through what remained of the street running up the middle of the ghost town, beyond it to the woods, where he had to dismount and lead his horse through the dense underbrush, as the path that had once been there was long gone.

A short distance into the woods was a steep dip, at the bottom of which was a cave, the mouth of it wide and towering, like a natural great hall or temple sanctuary. The founders of the town had turned it into a beautiful grotto, though now the benches, fountain, and other touches were, like everything, succumbing to the surrounding forest.

Sitting on what remained of one of the benches was a figure in a long, dark green cloak trimmed in fur that had been dyed to match, and lined in additional cream-colored wool for added warmth. The hood was up, giving no indication of their identity, though the slightness of the figure made him think woman.

Davrin had never been much with a sword, but he did well enough with his knives when there was no avoiding a fight, though the few he'd been in had been routing would-be thieves while he was walking about late at night or in the earliest hours of the morning.

The figure didn't react, not even to look up, as Davrin crunched his way to the grotto.

He took the bench opposite, awkwardly planted between an overenthusiastic tree root and a tangle of ivy.

The figure pulled down the cowl covering most of their face.

"Not what I expected, or would have even guessed if given fifty tries," Davrin said. Ever cautious of eavesdroppers, he kept his voice pitched low and said, "My lord."

Princess Korena chuckled softly. "Well met. Thank you for coming."

"I could hardly refuse such an intriguing invitation. I hope there is an explanation here at the end of my journey?"

"May I speak frankly?"

"My lord, I would be grateful. Most of my life is spent speaking sideways and in riddles. Frankness would be refreshing."

"His Majesty is a growing problem, and his

little thugs are bringing matters swiftly to a boiling point. I worry what they will do with this challenge, or worse, what they'll do to disrupt it, since King Rorlen's favorite can hardly be seen losing a challenge that accuses him of murder. I admire your bravery to face him despite the odds, and I'm pleased that Sir Cimar stepped up for you."

"It's an honor I do not merit," Davrin replied softly. "Sir Cimar is one of a kind."

"I agree, but you do yourself a disservice by dismissing your own merit. But we'll leave that for another time. There is something I want to share with you, but it requires absolute discretion."

"You have it, my lord. Always."

She smiled faintly, something in it bittersweet and longing. It faded after a moment, and she somberly continued, "His Majesty is dying. Worse, the healers tell me he is likely to start going mad—has already, in very minor ways, but he is going to worsen exponentially, likely over the course of months, but possibly it will take only weeks."

Davrin inhaled sharply through his nostrils. That was an alarming bit of news for the crown princess to share with a minor, if respected, diplomat. "I assume you want my help regarding the matter?"

"Yes. First and foremost, it is vital you win this challenge. I will support you as much as possible, but there's only so much I can do without drawing attention and risking everything. I must have Tekker and Grayne dishonored and thrown out of court before my father begins to collapse entirely. I worry what power he will give them before I am able to wrest it all away. If you win, he'll have no choice but to throw them out, and that will solve a great many problems before they begin. Your timing is fortuitous, though I realize you did not do this for me."

"I have always believed strongly in efficiency, my lord. The more problems that can be solved by a single action, the better. Have every faith that Sir Cimar and I will fight to the death to see Ballior is avenged and those two left in ruin. What else did you need of me?"

She offered another soft smile, this one far warmer, a hint of amusement in it. "You, actually, my lord."

Davrin frowned. "I do not follow."

"I am being pressured to marry; I have been for some time."

Davrin's confusion turned to shock. "You cannot be saying what I think you're saying."

She laughed, muffling the sound with her hand. "I am saying precisely that. I need a good man to be my prince consort. Someone who understands the kingdom, and more importantly, understands people. Who can help me lead without attempting to cast me aside like some courtly decoration."

"You need no man to rule," Davrin replied. "Anyone who thinks otherwise is a bloody fool. I still don't understand why you're choosing me."

"You know people. You have connections around the world that are worth a kingdom all on their own. You are loyal, and ambitious without being greedy or foolish. I have faith you would rule with me, not for me. People like you and trust you, and many are holding you in awe right now for daring to go against Lord Tekker, which basically equates to going directly against His Majesty. I've had my eye on you for some time, but I'd hoped to approach the matter more slowly, give us both time to decide if that would indeed work for both of us. But I am running out of time, so I am afraid the question must be put to you now, and you will not be able to take more than a few days to ponder it."

"I'll have an answer for you tomorrow. How should I send it?"

Removing her gloves, Korena removed a ring that was far too big for her finger but looked as though it would fit Davrin just fine. "If you agree to marry me, wear that to dinner tomorrow night, or sooner if you decide more quickly than that. If you decide against it, stow the ring in some other object and have it returned to me."

"I understand, my lord."

"Good. We'll talk more later once your decision is made. I bid you good day, my lord."

"My lord," Davrin replied, and rose. Retrieving his horse, he retraced his steps out of the woods, mounting when he reached the town.

He rode off in a daze, half-convinced he was dreaming or had taken a severe knock to the head. Not if his life depended on it would he have ever guessed the crown princess had been eyeing him for marriage. At best, if he'd thought about her at all, it would be that she might appoint him to a council position once she was on the throne.

But marriage? Prince Consort Davrin Dweller-by-the-Sea? No, his name would change with marriage. He'd be Prince Consort Davrin Highrow, Duke of Starfast, Earl of Broken Cliff, and Voice of the Council. And so much more besides. That was a dizzying rise in power. He pulled out the ring Korena had given him and finally looked it over.

A handsome piece, brilliant gold and set with a beautiful blue hawk's eye in an oval cut. It was a mark of the Order of the Osprey, a private circle of advisors and protectors founded by Her Highness and funded solely by her. Even her father had nothing to do with it. Membership to the order was secretive, and little was known about it outside its very close circle. So far as he knew, only nine others wore the rings, including Her Highness.

He tucked it away again, shifting his thoughts to more mundane matters as the dull journey carried on.

Sleet began to fall as the city came into view, and he hurried the horse as much as he dared. By the time he reached the inn, he was frozen and cranky. Handing off his horse to an equally miserable looking stable hand, he hastened into the building, where he gladly stripped out of his soaked outer wear and dumped it off on a woman who looked mollified by the coins he handed her for the trouble.

In the dining hall, more coins got him plenty of hot food and warm ale, along with a glass of whiskey to get the warming-up process started briskly. He drank that down in a smooth swallow, then set to work on the bread, venison, and beans set before him.

He hadn't been there long when the girl he'd hired stepped into the room, probably not the first time she'd checked to see if he was there, without sitting around forever with a bunch of packages drawing attention.

Lifting a hand to catch her eye, he beckoned her over and called for a drink. "Thank you. I hope you finished before this awful weather started."

"I did, thank you, my lord." She handed him a small package, the kind that generally came from a healer, containing a powder or bottled tincture. Inside, however, would be a key to a private room where his goods were being safely stored.

He took the package and tucked it away.

"Staying here to avoid the weather or did you want to head home?"

"Best be getting home. There's lots of extra baking to be done for the frost fair, and I'll be needed."

"Let me finish my meal and secure my purchases, and I'll give you a ride home. We'll still be miserable, but we'll get there faster."

"I'd be grateful, my lord. Thank you."

He called for more ale for them both and additional food, which she seemed surprised and delighted by. A gamble on his part, but he'd rarely seen anyone who wasn't glad to have more food, especially in winter.

An hour or so later, they were on their way, his cloak big enough to bundle both of them up fairly well, which was good, because hers was decent but not great. The trip to the castle was wretched and took longer than usual, but thankfully was still faster than attempting to walk ever would have been. When they arrived, he sent her bustled off with his cloak while he hastened on to his rooms shivering to death.

Someone had been thoughtful enough to see his room was nice and toasty, the crackling fire the best sound he'd heard all day. They'd hung his dressing robe near it, and he gladly abandoned his wet, icy clothes in favor of dry ones, shrugging into the robe with a groan.

Food was set out, a small plate of pies, cheese, and fruit that would keep if he didn't eat it immediately. Sitting in his chair, he stretched out his legs to thaw his poor feet and sipped at a glass of brandy. He set the ring Korena had given him next to the tray of food, then rested his head against the back of the chair and closed his eyes.

A few minutes later, he was stirred from a light doze by a rapping on his door and called for the knocker to enter. Two men bustled in carrying his packages. When they'd settled them on his trunks as directed, he beckoned them over and gave each a couple of coins. "Thank you."

"Milord," they chorused, and bowed before slipping back out of the room.

Left alone again, he worked slowly on the food and a second glass of brandy, worrying the ring the whole while.

Could he do it? For all he was used to wielding some measure of royal authority when he was abroad, it was something else entirely to think that someday he might be the one granting royal authority to speak for *him.*

Ballior would laugh if he was still here and tell him to do it. He was such a good, loyal friend he'd probably find reasons that Davrin should have always been the first choice, right from the start. Ballior always had possessed more faith and confidence—in himself and others—than anyone Davrin had ever met.

Thinking of Ballior brought a sharp pang. If he were still alive, Davrin would have made him Consort's Champion in a moment. They'd have been a good team, working alongside the princess—queen—and her champion.

Which of course brought his mind to Cimar. If he married Korena, he would have to forsake any feeble hope of speaking to Cimar of his feelings once and for all. But then, given their respective roles, it was not like they could have been lovers anyway. Would Cimar want to be a royal champion? It would suit him, if he did not want to return to his archives.

He'd never ached more for a real friend, someone he could speak with in confidence about this. All the overwhelming possibilities, good and bad, that would come if he agreed to marry Korena.

When he's finished his meal and brandy, Davrin stoked the fire, hung his robe up, and climbed into bed. The sheets were chilly but warmed quickly as he pulled the curtains and encased himself in a cocoon of wool and linen.

It was a couple of hours early for bed yet, but he was too cold and exhausted to do much else, and it was too dark anyway. Burrowing into the bedding, finding a comfortable position, he closed his eyes and tried to rest. Unfortunately, it was some time before he was able to, mind spinning between worries over Cimar and struggling to decide if he wanted to marry a future queen.

CHAPTER FOUR

"Holy tits, it's cold out here," Lee said. He held out his arm, covered in the special leather bracer, and Valor landed with one of her piercing cries. Lee drew her in close, pulling his cloak up to keep her protected from the brutal weather.

"I'm surprised you can still feel anything after all the hours we spent flying." Cimar rolled his shoulders and stretched his aching muscles, which weren't happy with him after all the flying, shifting, and bitter cold.

All around them was snow and ice, so deep and crusted over they could walk on it and pass the tops of some trees. Heavens forbid they go through it. The world was white, from top to bottom, and the wind carried a relentless wind that sapped warmth and will to live. "Let's get somewhere warm. You said you saw something from the sky?"

"This way," Lee said, testing his snowshoes before settling his pack and heading off. He had a sense of direction like Cimar had never seen before.

Pulling up his face cover, Cimar followed,

and onward they trudged for what felt like hours but was probably only a half hour at most. Throughout, the sky grew steadily darker, until he feared they'd either be digging into the snow for shelter or trudging by moonlight. Neither option was pleasant, though hiding in the snow would at least be warmer than the trudging.

They came to a stop right as the weak sunlight was surrendering its last rays to the dark, in front of a derelict cabin that barely deserved the word. When the door wouldn't give, Cimar removed his snowshoes and gave it a solid kick, which thankfully did the trick.

Inside, the cabin smelled of disuse but mercifully nothing worse. A handful of rodent skeletons littered the floor; Lee made quick work of them while Cimar set to building a fire. Valor flew to perch on the back of a chair, seemingly content to preen her ruffled feathers while watching them.

When the fire was going, Cimar stripped off his heavy gloves and got his hands warmed so he could make dinner without fumbling and dropping everything.

Lee, in his usual brisk, efficient way, set to work stowing their things for the night, cleaning the floor enough to be workable, and getting their bedrolls set up. He also got Valor fed, laughing as she nibbled on his fingers in thanks.

Though Cimar was still far from pleased about the unfair quest, he was grateful he'd been able to fly them here. Otherwise, the horses would be a burden, and they probably would have been forced to turn them back or abandon them. Valor had flown alongside them most of the way, and ridden in Lee's arms when she'd needed a break. He'd expected more difficulty with her regarding his shifted form, but Valor hadn't seemed to care.

Stretching out his muscles again, Cimar finally set to work on dinner, pulling out jerky and tack, and using the special powders he'd brought along to make a thin broth that would warm them up. He also got a kettle going, though that required going out to scoop piles of snow first, which ruined all his efforts at getting warm.

While the water and soup heated, they sat bundled in their cloaks gnawing at the jerky. "So what do you think we'll find, Lee? Violence or plague?"

"Plague. Let's just hope it's finished the job." Lee took an unenthusiastic bite of jerky. As jerky went, it wasn't bad—venison, and well-seasoned. But almost anything was better than jerky and tack.

Cimar chewed another strip of his own, casting a watchful eye on the pots over the fire. If it hadn't been clear from the start, it was brutally clear now that His Majesty was hoping they'd die up here, or at least get trapped long enough they lost the challenge by default.

If only the winds hadn't kept him from flying all the way to Castle Bone itself. But this high up, especially in this weather, the wind could practically toss around boulders. The only thing Cimar dreaded more than plague was an avalanche. They might survive the former; they definitely would not survive the latter.

Lee poured them tea as the water boiled, and a short time later the broth was done as well, which made eating the rock-hard tack a thousand times easier. It wasn't a terribly exciting meal, but it was warm and filling, which was all that mattered in the end.

When they'd finished eating, Cimar took care of cleaning up, leaving Lee to settle on his bedroll. Instead of lying down to sleep, however, Lee sat with his legs folded in front of him, elbows on his knees, hands close but not quite cupped. Every now and then something seemed to spark or shimmer within them, like glowbugs caught in the summer.

Training exercises, though not nearly as rigorous as he would normally do, since there wasn't space, and he probably didn't have the mental or physical strength at the moment, not after the long day they'd had.

Magic came in two forms: those born with the rare ability to shift, and those who could call upon their own life force and manifest it in various ways, most often light or fire, though in days long past it was said there were mages who could nigh on control the elements. The precise science behind it wasn't well known; most were content to call it the will of the gods and leave well enough alone.

Leonine was particularly adept with his magic, at a level Cimar hadn't seen outside of some of the oldest women in the abbey and a couple of knights long retired. Knights generally preferred to rely solely on their physical prowess, considering magic a sort of cheat. Most of that attitude seemed to stem from envy and resentment, but it was deeply ingrained in knightly culture. Lee, however, was no fool. He had an advantage and he used it, and Castle Bone was likely going to require every advantage they could muster.

"Don't overwork yourself," Cimar said around a yawn. "Get some rest."

Lee smiled faintly, a sign he would listen shortly, and Cimar left him to it. Settling on his bedroll, he wrapped his cloak snuggly around him and was asleep almost immediately.

~~*

The morning brought no relief from the snow, but the wind had died down, which made a world of difference as they traveled. Valor launched into the sky with a cry, clearly pleased to spread her wings again. Cimar could have flown them the rest of the way, but he didn't want to risk the wind kicking back up, and arriving on foot would give them a better chance at the element of surprise.

They traveled steadily, pausing occasionally for rest and slightly longer for lunch. Not long after they resumed the journey, the castle came into view. It was nestled in a valley, close to a pond with a churning waterfall. When the castle had been constructed, it looked as though they'd dug out a moat that used the pond to fill it, which would prove useful in a number of ways if they weren't stupid enough to let the water contaminate with sewage and other refuse.

"No smoke, no movement of any sort," Lee said. "I guess we weren't really expecting any, though."

"I'm more concerned there's no livestock. The reindeer might have scattered after a bit, if plague wiped everyone out, but the musk oxen would have stayed close, since there's room aplenty and reliable food and water here. Plague or bandits, there's no reason for all the livestock to be missing. Keep alert, Lee, and be ready to run."

"Yes, sir," Lee said quietly.

Cimar led the way down the hill toward the keep, making certain his sword could be easily drawn if necessary. He'd come prepared to roust bandits or burn the remains of plague victims. He had not come prepared for a mystery.

The wind picked up slightly as they reached the valley floor, and Cimar gagged at the stench it brought: death, decay. Not really a shock that everyone was dead, but according to what he'd been told, these people should have been dead for months. Their bodies should be frozen, unable to leave much in the way of stench until the spring thaw.

"This grows increasingly ominous," he said. "Let's ready our bows."

Lee immediately stopped and swung his pack down, swiftly untying the bows he'd secured to it and digging out string from one of the many pockets. He handed one length to Cimar and used the second to string his own bow.

The wood didn't like the cold, but Cimar paid well for his armor and weapons, and these bows had been specially treated to endure extreme climate. They'd be stiffer and slightly more prone to breaking, but in expert hands they'd do well enough, and neither he nor Lee was an amateur.

Lee favored a short bow, which broadly was more useful. Cimar, though, had grown up learning the long bow and had never been able to part with it.

When their arrows were unpacked and in the quivers at their hips, they resumed walking.

"What do you think it could be?" Lee asked. "How could the smell be that strong? Surely there aren't any people or animals around in enough numbers to be that… fresh."

Cimar's jaw tightened as he weighed possibilities, but only one stood out bright and sharp in his mind. "I don't think it's the bodies that smell that way. I think that stench emanates from the problem itself. If I am correct, Castle Bone has been overrun by a lindworm."

"Well. Fuck."

"Precisely."

As they drew closer, the stench grew so bad that Lee had to pause to throw up, and he remained a sickly green the rest of the journey to the castle.

They stopped several paces shy of the drawbridge, and it took everything Cimar possessed not to throw up his own breakfast.

Lindworms were ravenous beasts, gigantic serpents with a seemingly bottomless appetite that preferred their food to be alive when it was swallowed. They were covered with thick, nearly impervious scales that were a deceptively beautiful silvery-white, with a head that closely resembled that of dragons to the untrained eye. They had bloodred eyes and venomous fangs that paralyzed victims so they'd go easily into the gullet, where they'd be slowly digested.

The worst thing about lindworms was that they had once been human. Shifters who got stuck in their shifted form and went mad, or otherwise corrupt, and began to shift again, growing and shedding and growing until all that remained was a monster.

Someone in the castle had been a shifter, and something had happened to turn them into a lindworm, and in their ravening they'd consumed the other inhabitants, all the people they'd called peer and friend and family.

"I've only ever read about them," Lee said, voice shaking slightly. "Never thought I'd actually encounter one. Do you really think that's what we're up against?"

"Unfortunately, I do. One of the tell-tale marks is that they smell like rotting corpses." He didn't bother to elaborate that most of that stench came from the fact lindworms perpetually had bodies rotting inside them. "The complete lack of anything living is another tell." He handed Lee his bow and extended his left arm, where he wore the leather bracer. He whistled sharply, high and piercing, and far above them Valor gave an answering cry as she made her way down. "Get a message ready."

A few minutes later Valor alighted on his arm and accepted the food he offered. While she ate, Lee got the message affixed to her leg.

When she was done eating and the message secure, Cimar launched her back into the air and then gave the series of whistles that ordered her to return home. An answering cry, and then she was swiftly lost to the sky.

"That's that," Cimar said. Lee held out his bow, but Cimar shook his head and first reached up to remove the white collar around his throat. He always felt strange without it, but there might not be time enough to remove it later. Everything else he wore, armor included, would give way to the shift, but the specially made leather collar risked choking him if it wasn't removed ahead of time.

Stowing the collar, he took back his bow. "Hang back a few paces, Lee. Keep our rear covered but be prepared to run the moment I tell you. Let's work our way around the castle, see if we can get in through a side passage, find some high ground. Our only advantage right now is that lindworms are large; it won't be able to just slither through most of the hallways around here."

"Could slither up a column though," Lee muttered, but fell into step a few paces behind him as directed, keeping his bow at the ready, though arrows would be useless unless they struck its softer underbelly or right in one of its eyes.

They found entry by way of the kitchens, though Lee puked again at the pile of remains scattered there, bits and pieces of people and livestock in various stages of decay.

"I always thought I had a strong stomach," Lee said miserably.

"This is infinitely worse than anything you'd see on a battlefield or even a plague-felled city. No one should ever have to bear witness to this level of... gleeful, ravening violence. Now be silent, unless the matter is urgent. Lindworms aren't known for their hearing, but they aren't deaf either. Worse, they have an acute sense of smell."

Lee nodded and nocked an arrow.

They pressed on, the stench growing worse with every step. Never in his life had Cimar wanted so badly to be anywhere else in the world.

When he found a set of stairs, he swiftly climbed them, Lee behind him. They traveled the hallways slowly, frequently gagging. Bodies were everywhere—lords, servants, livestock, pets. It was clear a great many of them had been injured, either by the lindworm or in an ensuing panic, and died of their injuries up here where they couldn't be eaten. A blessing of sorts, but still a cruel and miserable way to die.

If they managed to survive this, the rest of the challenge would be laughably easy, though frankly he thought defeating a lindworm should qualify for an automatic win.

They'd be fully within their rights to retreat and come back with a greater force, but he also wouldn't put it past His Majesty to still use the retreat as an excuse to call the challenge a loss and see he was awarded no points. Cimar would be damned before he let that happen.

He just wished his quest had been a little bit easier than this.

As they turned a corner, he could see the rafters and tapestries of the great hall. So this was the mezzanine. Signaling to Lee, he crept up to the balustrade—and barely choked back a scream.

"Oh, god," Lee said on a sob, sinking to his

knees and clinging to the balusters, head pressed against them as he bit back the rest of his sounds.

Cimar had to wipe his own eyes on the sleeves of his tunic before he could take a second, more thorough look at the devastating nightmare below.

Nothing remained of the great hall but ruins—and corpses. So many corpses. Livestock. Knights. Women. He had to turn away for a moment after spying children. It was like the lindworm had lost its mind, fallen into a frenzy, and been more interested in the killing than the eating. Or maybe it was an outlier and preferred carrion to fresh meat. Whatever the reason, the results would haunt Cimar's sleep for the rest of his life.

In the middle of the hall, curled up in a nest made of fabric and destroyed furniture, was the monster itself. Its scales looked like they'd been carved from moonlight and opals, and Cimar could just see the crown of spikes on its head that was the main difference in skull between dragons and lindworms.

The damn thing was also vastly more enormous than he'd anticipated. It slept like the dead, only the barest rise and fall of its coiled body to indicate it was, in fact, alive. Cimar did not want to know how much bigger it would seem once it started moving.

Whatever happened, it must have happened fast, that no one had been able to get word out. That no survivors had found their way to the royal castle. But what of all the messengers? That was an easy one, though, even if it further curdled his stomach: they'd probably been hunted. If not for the fact it was asleep, it was entirely possible the lindworm might have gotten to them before they ever reached the castle.

"I've never heard of a lindworm that was this big. This is far more than the two of us can handle. I could shift, but that has risks of its own that I'd rather not take unless unavoidable. Retreat is our best option."

"Agreed," Lee said grimly. "Let's get out of here." He stood slowly, then bent to retrieve his dropped bow—but the string, still taut, caught on a bit of rubble and sent it tumbling between two balusters. It crashed into a pile of skeletons below, sending bones and other debris scattering across the floor.

Waking the lindworm, who growled softly at the noise—and then roared as it smelled fresh meat.

"Fuck," Cimar said.

Lee choked out, "I'm sorry," between sobs.

"Run, Lee. I'm the only chance we've got at facing this thing. Go back to the cabin. If I don't rejoin you by tomorrow at sunset, do your best to make it home without me. Understand?"

Though he looked like he wanted to protest, Cimar had taken Lee as a squire because he was smart, and smart sometimes meant taking the option that hurt.

"I'll be fine. Go."

Lee hugged him tightly, then ran back the way they'd come right as the Lindworm rose up to get a better look at its prey. How, or if, Lindworms could see, at least the way people saw, was still a subject for debate. Like most snakes and serpents, it relied most on its sense of smell.

Cimar discarded all that he could, preferring to ruin as few of his belongings as possible, even if the chances he'd be able to retrieve them later were slim.

When he was mostly naked, the Lindworm drawing far too close for comfort, he took a deep breath—and as he released it, let his magic have him.

The change hurt for a split second before the magic dulled the pain, like a thousand hot knives searing right through him. Then there was only the strange sensations of changing: cracking, tearing, growing, in size and in body parts, as his shifted form had two hearts, two stomachs, and other alterations to accommodate his enormous size.

Most importantly right now, his shifted form possessed a fire sac.

The lindworm launched right as he finished changing, venom dripping and flying from its fangs.

Cimar roared as it latched onto his throat,

choking hard enough to bruise but the fangs not quite able to puncture his scales. Not this time, anyway, but it was only a matter of time if he didn't find a way to end this quickly. He braced his back legs on the wall and shoved off with all his might. He didn't get much momentum, as the wall cracked and crumbled, but it was enough to send them tumbling back down into the great hall proper, scattering bones and wood and other rubble.

Snorting hard, Cimar picked himself up and shook. Across the hall, by what was left of the main doors, the lindworm hissed and coiled into a striking pose.

Cimar hadn't wanted to fight this way because it was taxing and would have been dangerous for Lee, and the Lindworm would get through his scales much easier than he'd get through its. But there was no help for it now, so if he had to bring the whole damn castle down, that was what he'd do.

The lindworm sprang, and Cimar whipped around, bringing his tail up and slamming it into the lindworm before its fangs could land. It crashed into—more through—a wall, and the entire castle shook as it lost some vital support.

Guess he *was* going to bring the whole damn castle down.

As the lindworm disentangled itself from the shattered remains of the wall, Cimar pulled in a deep lungful of air, then hitched slightly, activating the fire sac. As he breathed out, the special fluid in his sac rushed up his throat and caught fire as it reached his mouth, where his rough tongue scraped specialized teeth that sparked.

The lindworm caught the line of fire right in the face, causing it to shriek and writhe as the flames burned—melted—its eyes.

Cimar cut the flames, and as the smoke cleared, he saw he'd also destroyed the lindworm's tongue—most of the inside of its mouth. It shrieked and wailed with pain, but blind now in more ways than one, there wasn't much it could do.

Not that didn't try anyway. It lashed out blindly, shrieking, screaming, venom flying everywhere, swinging its head to try and get Cimar with the crown of spikes, bringing up its tail to get him with the even longer, nastier spikes there.

Cimar spewed more fire, until he had nothing left, and the entire great hall was aflame. The lindworm had nowhere to go, too wounded and panicky to realize its scales would allow it to slither right through them and out into the cooling snow.

Plunging through the flames, Cimar whacked it hard with his tail, sending it crashing to the ground. Then he leaned down and sank his massive teeth into the soft underbelly, right at the throat, ripping and tearing, holding fast through the lindworm's death throes, letting go only when it went still, and the rancid odor of excrement told him the body had voided itself in death.

Letting go, Cimar shook himself, hating the vile taste lingering in his mouth, and looked around. The easiest way out was the main doors, so that was where he headed—then stopped at the last minute and went back to the lindworm. Latching onto its throat again, he dragged it out into the snow, well away from the rapidly burning castle.

Rushing back inside, he leveraged himself up and over the mezzanine, tearing and throwing, until he found his little stash all the way at the back where he'd tucked it behind a statue. Awkwardly, he scooped it all up into his mouth as best he could, though there was a gauntlet that fell that he couldn't retrieve without losing more of the pile.

Forsaking the poor gauntlet, he clamped down tightly on the rest of his gear and scrabbled like mad to get out of the castle. Dragons might be immune to fire, but nothing and no one was immune to having heavy stones fall on their head.

Outside, he spat out his clothes, armor, and weapons near the dead lindworm, then huddled over his belongings protectively as he watched the castle burn.

He dozed here and there, needing the rest if he was going to make it to the cabin to fetch Lee, back to the castle, and then home after that.

By sunrise, the castle had mostly burned itself out. There were some smoldering bits, but the snow and sleet would take care of it long before it managed to burn any of the trees—if it even could, given how frozen they were.

Heaving to his feet, he then launched into the air and flew back to the cabin.

He'd barely landed when Lee burst out of it. "You're alive! Thank the gods!" He looked near to tears as he rushed over to help Cimar as he shifted back. "Are you all right?"

"Exhausted but fine," Cimar said. "Come on, I need your help skinning the lindworm, then we need to pack it and my belongings for travel. Get your things."

"You should rest a bit."

"I'll rest when we're home, especially after I see the look on King Rorlen's face when we return weeks early—when we return at all, at that."

Lee frowned, but with a sigh ran back to the cabin and was back in a few minutes. Groaning, Cimar shifted again and took them back to the castle—well, castle ruins, now.

Skinning the lindworm was difficult, grisly work, not least of all because it had once been a human being. On some level, it seemed wrong. On the other hand, there was nothing finer for armor and weapons than lindworm scales, and the lindworm hardly needed them anymore. After all the destruction and death it had caused, it could give up its scales.

Far more importantly, it was incontrovertible proof that he'd slain a lindworm. Let Tekker and Grayne choke on that.

When their grisly task was complete, they washed away as much of the blood and ichor as they could with the surrounding snow, then carefully rolled it, using scraps of cloth they scrounged up to tie it securely. Cimar would be able to carry it to where they'd left their horses, and from there they could hire a cart and oxen to take it all the way to the castle.

In roughly a day, maybe two, he'd be winner of the quest challenge. One down, two to go.

CHAPTER FIVE

The worst part of anything was the waiting. There were people who swore anticipation was the ultimate high, and maybe in some respects it was—certainly sex benefited from it—but for the most part, Davrin hated the waiting.

He could do it, better than most in fact. His job often relied on outwaiting the other party. Patience was everything in diplomacy; it was also a lot of hurry up and wait. So he'd mastered the skill.

That didn't mean he'd ever learned to enjoy it.

Especially the waiting that came after receiving a dire message. Like that his champion and secret love of his life had learned the reason for Castle Bone's silence was a *lindworm.* Davrin never thought he'd wish for a day when he heard the cause of a problem was plague, but well, that day was here.

The message had said to take no action until further word was received—or not received, in three full sunrises—which did not make the waiting less maddening. Not in the slightest. Davrin had not been able to sleep since he'd been summoned to Her Highness's public chambers and informed of the message.

All he'd been able to do was keep vigil, pausing occasionally to recite prayers he barely recalled and most often could not care less about.

The snow had resumed around sunrise, muffling the world like a blanket and likely slowing the progress of further messengers or, gods willing, Cimar and Lee.

A lindworm. What were the chances of that? It took no small effort to get from human to lindworm. What poor bastard had made that journey, and how many people had died at its end? Davrin could only be grateful answering those questions was not his problem.

He watched, fingers gripping the railing tightly, as a slight figure on an enormous plow horse was let through the portcullis and made their way quickly up the road to the keep proper. As hastily as snow and hidden ice permitted at any rate.

What would some farm boy be doing coming all the way here on a day like this? Bringing a message? But of what? Davrin did not dare get his hopes up. Instead he dismissed the farm boy and kept his eyes further afield, ever hoping to see a familiar figure appear in the lazily falling snow, likely battered and bruised but alive. Or maybe they'd had the sense to not try to take on the lindworm after all and had made a strategic retreat. It would take a full force, or several large, well-trained shifters, to take on a lindworm. Even someone like Grayne, his hellhound form so enormous one paw would dwarf Davrin's head, would struggle. It would take several hellhounds, or something as rare as a cockatrice or dragon, and even they would need a large dose of luck.

The sound of footsteps in his chambers drew his attention, and he turned sharply, annoyed with himself for failing to notice the knocking. A servant wearing Korena's crest curtsied. "Beg pardon, Lord Dweller-by-the-Sea, but Her Highness bid me fetch you to her chambers with all haste."

Davrin's heart kicked up. Could the farmer on the horse have been related to Cimar after all? It seemed too good to be true. "Of course." He strode into his room, closing the doors to the balcony behind him and locking them, brushing off snow as he went over to the vanity table near his bed. There, he picked up the ring he'd been intending to wear to dinner that night. May as well wear it now, and gods did he hope he was making the right decision.

His heart hurt at the way Cimar would be really and truly lost to him forever, but even if there had ever really been a chance for them, a chance Cimar returned his affections, some things were simply more important, no matter how unfair that seemed.

Ready, he followed the servant through the halls, to where she predictably stopped at the door to Korena's smaller public receiving room, where she received nobles, important guests, and others of rank. She escorted him inside and left him there—alone, surprisingly. There was no sign at all that Korena had been or would be there. She must have been abruptly called away to something else, or not yet been able to escape. But then why not send a message? Another servant?

A soft creak interrupted his thoughts, and he turned to see one of the paintings on the far wall swing open, revealing the woman who'd delivered the peregrine, Lady Aliara. She was beautiful enough she stood out in a castle filled with beautiful people. She had a sturdy body, the sort that lent itself well to combat, carrying the weight of armor. Her skin was a warm, yellow-toned brown, with freckles across her cheeks and broad nose that added a winsomeness to her stern demeanor. In another life, she might have been a general or queen. Her black hair was woven into several medium-sized braids that were then pulled back into an intricate knot, secured with an ornate gold hairpin decorated with rubies that matched her scarlet gown and the chatelaine affixed to her girdle. "Good afternoon, my lord."

"My lady."

She smiled faintly and motioned for him to follow. Bemused, he climbed the steep step up into what proved to be a narrow hallway, lit only by the light spilling from the room at the far end. As she closed the door to the receiving room, it grew darker still. Probably for the best he could see next to nothing, given his strong aversion to the sorts of things that liked to creepy around in dark, damp places.

He shuddered as what was unmistakably a spiderweb brushed his cheek and frantically brushed it and any possible spiders away. Ahead of him, Aliara walked in a way that said spiders were of no concern. Davrin was envious.

Though the tunnel was short, it felt like they walked for ages, until they spilled out of a door that proved to be hidden by a tapestry this time. From there, she led him through what seemed to be the front room of Korena's private chambers to a small, private library, though currently it was overtaken by the embroidery project she and probably several others were working on, a vibrant blue gown clearly intended for some formal occasion.

Aliara took her seat and resumed her work as Korena set her own section of the gown aside. Her eyes fell to Davrin's hands, uncovered and clear of his cloak. Looking up, she smiled, warm and bright and unmistakably relieved. "Good afternoon, dear fiancé. I've just received news you've been wanting to hear."

"Cimar and his squire are all right then?"

She rose and crossed over to him, taking one of his hands and wrapping it reassuringly in her own. "Yes. Your champion is none to be trifled with—we already knew that, but he's set to become legend. According to the lad who came bearing the message, they will be here by nightfall, weather permitting, along with a cart carrying the lindworm's skin."

"What!"

Korena laughed and let go of his hand.

"That is precisely what Her Highness said when the messenger first told us."

Korena shot Aliara a playfully reprimanding look. "You stop it."

Aliara grinned before turning her focus back to her sewing.

"Walk with me?" Korena asked.

"My honor," Davrin replied, and offered his arm.

She led him out of the library and out a door to what proved to be her private garden, covered in expensive glass and kept warm so herbs and other necessaries could be grown throughout the year. She could have easily filled it with roses and other indulgent plants to enjoy, but he wasn't surprised she instead put it to practical use. Korena had always put others before herself, the very opposite of her father.

Even in looks, they were disparate, for Korena had gotten all of hers from her mother: the light brown skin and dark, red-brown hair bound in twin plaits pinned up in knots, and the full, generous figure that men loved to speak crudely of when they thought no one of importance could overhear them, along with all the ways they'd love to 'make a real woman' of her.

Davrin had always kept his mouth tactfully shut, but the sudden realization that as prince consort he could finally put them in their place was delightful.

They came to a stop near a worktable, where someone had recently been cutting and bundling herbs and turning others into powder or paste. She let go of his arm and turned to face him. "What decided you?"

"Well, it's hard to complain about being offered such a position," he replied wryly. "More sincerely, it seemed like the right thing to do. You enumerated the reasons. Even after much careful contemplation, I can find no flaw. If you trust me to be your prince consort, then I am happy to be so, or at least try my very best."

She smiled, that warm, bright smile again that showed something—much—of the person behind the crown. "Then we've much to discuss, in the way of details, but I did want to go ahead and settle one matter for you, regarding the more intimate elements of our relationship."

"What matter is that?"

"I wanted to assure you that I would never expect you to sever your relationship with Sir Cimar. Aliara is my lover and beloved, and I would not part ways with her for any price. If that—" She faltered briefly, then rallied, "If that arrangement troubles you, then we can either part ways or both sever the romantic elements of our respective relationships. I would greatly prefer nobody have to do any such thing, if it's in our power to come to an arrangement much happier for all."

Davrin inhaled sharply. "I see. I think you're kind and generous, Your Highness, and I'd never dream of demanding you cease your relationship with Lady Aliara. I fear there is a misunderstanding here, though. Cimar and I are acquainted, and perhaps even friends after a fashion, but we've never been lovers."

Her brow furrowed, mouth turning down. "Really? But the way you two look at each other, the way he's stood for you as champion when he's turned away so many generous offers…"

"He never mentioned that," Davrin said softly. But of course Cimar wouldn't. He was in every way exactly what a knight should be. "I'll be frank, Highness—"

"I think you can use my name, under the circumstances," she said, lips twitching.

"Not unless you want to give the game away sooner than is safe."

She made a face. "Of course. That was foolish of me. But continue, please, my apologies."

"In all honesty, I wish Cimar was my lover. I've long thought of him in ways forbidden to me, but my duties and his marriage always kept me from making a fool of myself."

"I think too many rules are kept long after their purpose fades." She smiled, a hint of playfulness in it. "I also think you should perhaps be as honest with Sir Cimar as you are with me." Stepping in closer, she draped her arms around his neck. "You'll have husbandly duties to perform, my prince, but I trust you to know what you are about if you go seeking other beds when your presence isn't required in mine."

Davrin chuckled and slid an arm around her waist as she brushed a teasing kiss across his mouth. "If only all my duties were even half so pleasant. I'll be more than happy to serve, my queen." Which was true. Davrin was as attracted to women as he was men, and Korena was hardly a curse upon the eyes.

She did, in fact, feel rather nice pressed right up against him, nice enough that he'd make his feelings quite plain if she didn't step away soon.

"Well, that is one matter resolved, and rather easily," she replied.

"I'm generally only ever hard when and where it matters," Davrin replied, pleased when she laughed. "Was there anything else that required immediate discussion?"

"No, the rest is all details that can wait. I had simply wanted to reassure you that I wasn't expecting you to sever your relationship with Cimar and to tell you the truth of Aliara. I hope over time the four of us will come to a comfortable arrangement." Her eyes glittered. "Though first my fiancé must step up and acquire the lover."

"Not the strangest royal command I've ever been given, but certainly a close second."

She laughed again and took his arm when he offered, and they made their way from the garden.

"If I am to do as commanded, though, it would be better if his current marriage was severed once and for all." He related what little Cimar had told him of the matter, including King Rorlen's refusal to grant a severance.

"I'll take care of it," Korena replied, and sighed. "It's nice to occasionally have a problem with an easy solution."

As they reached the library, Aliara promptly cast aside her work, clearly not as absorbed in it as she'd seemed before. "Well?"

"Come here and kiss me, you fretful goose," Korena replied.

Aliara threw herself out of her chair and obeyed with enthusiasm. Davrin strove to behave honorably, and give them a moment, but it was damned difficult not to look his fill at a sight intoxicating enough people would surrender entire fortunes to enjoy it for mere minutes.

It also didn't take Korena telling him to see the two were deeply in love. But though Aliara was a suitable candidate in every other way, the heir to the throne was required to marry for heirs, and unless he was mistaken, neither Korena nor

Aliara possessed an essential component to that process.

Davrin silently bid his own essential component to behave.

When they finally drew apart, Aliara approached him and curtsied, then rose and tidied her hair and mussed dress. "Thank you for being so understanding, my lord." She winked. "Your Highness."

"That will take getting used to it," Davrin said. "Even in my most ambitious daydreams, my being royalty made no appearance. I am sorry it cannot be you, my lady."

She smiled, bittersweet but accepting. "What we have is far better than we dared to hope, and more than most will ever have. I was happy to learn Sir Cimar survived the lindworm. The other knights will have quite the time trying to outdo him at story time!"

"Oh, that reminds me," Korena replied, and reached into the pouch at her waist. "Your official ring, so you already have it whenever we announce it, or should there be an emergency so dire that confessing our engagement will help resolve the situation. Also a ring for Sir Cimar, who more than earned it by rising to the challenge."

Davrin took them as she held them out. One was an Order of the Osprey ring, Cimar's name carved inside. The other was a large, handsome, and heavy piece that dwarfed and dulled every other ring in his collection, and he had many, an assortment of official rings, heirlooms, and gifts.

This one was gold, set with a large square cut emerald framed by smaller diamonds and emeralds in an alternating pattern. The band was wide, completely covering his finger up to the first knuckle, and inside was carved the royal motto: *we will always rise, no matter how hard we might fall.*

It also tingled with old magic; likely once he put the ring on, there would be no taking it off his finger until death—or far nastier magic came along. He tucked them away in his own pouch. "I will pass it on when he arrives home tonight, and I vow I'll not betray your trust in me."

"If I suspected you would even consider it, I would have not given you that ring. It's been spelled to you already, so if another steals it and tries to wear it, they will sorely regret it—if they live."

"That is powerful magic." Especially given magic simply didn't show up often. The history books said it had once been far more prevalent, and shifting alongside it, but a bad combination of war, plague, and famine had wiped out entire swaths of the world, and those with magic or shifter blood had suffered the greatest losses. "I didn't know anyone in the castle was capable of that."

Korena winked. "Stay long enough, and you'll find out who."

Davrin laughed.

They all turned as a knock came at the far outer door, the visitor pounding so hard it probably echoed down the entire wing.

"That doesn't sound good," Aliara replied. She gathered her skirts and hastened off, and returned a moment later, her face gone ashen. "Korena, you must come at once. It's about your father."

"Shit," Korena said, sharp and succinct. "Davrin—"

"I'll remain in here, and when there is a moment to slip away discreetly, I shall do so."

Korena nodded and departed, Aliara at her side.

Davrin moved to the mostly closed door, well out of sight of roaming eyes but close enough he could hear what was happening, should it be something that required quick action.

The man who'd come to see them, one of King Rorlen's personal attendants, spoke in low tones, but he wasn't experienced enough at it somehow to keep the castle walls from carrying them.

His Majesty had thrown a serious fit just minutes ago, behaving like some wild animal, throwing things around the room, wounding several people in the process. All of them servants, but no matter how discreet they all swore they would be, one of them would eventually run their mouth—for the thrill, from booze, or for good old-fashioned bribery.

Korena dismissed the attendant, and Aliara closed the door behind him, leaning against it and sharing a look of stark exhaustion and fear with Korena.

Davrin opened the library door and stepped out into the main room. "I'm guessing this is far more than a normal tantrum."

"Yes," Korena said, turning. "It's one of the signs of the madness, but it wasn't supposed to manifest for weeks yet, even months. Barley, the attendant, said the healer suspects it may have simply been a bad reaction to one of the medications they're trying, but he won't know for certain for a couple of days. But if the worst possible scenario has come to pass, and my father is already progressing deeply into madness..."

He wouldn't be fit to rule, fit to continue overseeing the challenge, and Korena couldn't do it in his place now they were engaged—and she couldn't break the engagement without opening the way for countless others, like Lord Tekker, who'd had King Rorlen's support for years and all the power and back alley methods he needed to secure enough support to literally force Korena's hand.

No one could force a crown princess, a queen, to say yes. But they could make the cost of her 'no' devastating.

"If we must call off the challenge, then so be it," Davrin said, even as his heart broke to surrender his one and only chance to obtain justice for Ballior. "The kingdom is more important than the honor of a dead man, and if we marry now, as I suspect you're plotting, then there won't be much Tekker can really do in the end."

"We have time yet, if precious little," Korena said. "My father's healer said he needed a couple of days. In the meantime, they are making every effort to spread that the medicine *is* the cause for his temper, and it was for something harmless." She sighed. "In the meantime, I will prepare everything should we have to marry in haste. Keep that ring on you at all times, Lord Dweller-by-the-Sea. You bear it, you are hereby authorized to act on behalf of the royal throne. Your word is my word."

"Witnessed," Lady Aliara said softly. "Come, I'll escort you back to your chambers."

They received curious looks as they walked, but it was neither strange nor suspicious that the best diplomat in the castle would be speaking with Her Highness, so any rumors people tried to stir up wouldn't last very long—especially when King Rorlen was currently far more interesting to gossip about by far. By this point, they probably didn't even remember Cimar would be returning soon with a lindworm skin.

Back in his room, he sat at his writing desk and focused on the never-ending pile of correspondence. The worst was that this was simply the stuff that couldn't be handled by his assistant. Otherwise, Davrin would likely spend the whole of his life right there, sending reply after reply after reply. People thought diplomacy was all fancy dinners and quiet, bitterly polite fights around large tables, and while those things certainly occurred, much of diplomacy was sending hundreds of carefully worded letters full of promises, threats, offers, giving or accepting favors, and being the go-between for all of the same. By the time any of them actually met in person, it was mostly to officially sign off—or unofficially sign off—on everything already agreed to.

He was more than a bit intimidated by how much more complicated this would all get when he was prince consort. The ring in his pouch weighed next to nothing, yet felt like he was carrying around a boulder.

When his brain simply could not handle a single word more, he put everything away, locked the desk, and went to read something relaxing instead. His meagre collection of books had been obtained slowly and carefully over the years, too costly and difficult to travel with for him to purchase lightly.

Thinking of books brought to mind Korena's impressive private library, though he would likely be too busy to avail himself of it often.

He looked around his chambers, where he'd lived for years, decades, off and on between his journeys abroad. The room was always here, awaiting his return, the servants ensuring that it was dusted and freshened, always bright and pleasant upon his arrival. Who would it go to when the room was no longer his? There'd be a whole list of people waiting for such an opportunity, and serious power play in the decision.

Perhaps—

The thought scattered as a pounding knock came at the door. Davrin strode over and yanked the door open, stared at the red-faced servant in the hall. "Yes?"

"Riders spotted down the road. Her Highness said to summon you to the great hall."

"Thank you." Davrin dismissed her and went to fetch the cloak he'd removed before settling into work, as the castle was miserably drafty no matter what attempts were made to keep it warm. It had been built for war, not for comfort, and King Rorlen had never put earnest effort, or even permission and funds, into changing that.

Heart pounding in his chest, anxiety warring with relief, he made his way swiftly through the castle to the great hall, where it looked like every last inhabitant had tried to cram in. No one had cared about the challenge, not really, but one lindworm and suddenly everyone was invested. Understanding and resentment warred in Davrin, but he tamped it all down and focused on what mattered: Cimar was nearly home, he'd won the first challenge, and beyond all that he'd just won enormous support and favoritism among the castle population. People were invested now, and that changed the entire shape of the game.

Korena beckoned to him from the royal dais, and Davrin pushed through the crowds to join her, bowing to King Rorlen and then to her, before obediently standing at her side. A courtesy, but later after the engagement was announced, people would look back on little things like this and wonder just how long they'd had an arrangement.

More likely, they'd claim they'd known, or at least suspected, all along, and attempt to out-do each other with brag after brag of the hints and details they and they alone had noticed. Davrin could predict nearly to the person what each of them would say.

King Rorlen seemed oddly subdued, more so than usual; the healer had probably given him a light sedative so there'd be no repeat of his earlier fit. A less arrogant man might have handed the matter over to his heir, but Rorlen had never lacked arrogance, unfortunately for everybody.

On Rorlen's left, Lord Tekker was as still and unreadable as stone. Standing behind and slightly to his left, Sir Grayne looked his usual rotten-lemon self. It didn't take a diplomat with years of experience to read the two men were livid with the way this first challenge had concluded. Grayne had been given a quest that amounted to a child's game, and before he had bothered to even begin, his rival returned with a lindworm skin. It was the sort of wild tale told by bards, and yet Cimar had made it reality.

The steward called for order, and when they were quiet, for everyone to move out of the way. People slowly, grumbling and sniping at one another as they vied to maintain a good position, cleared a path. They managed it just as the enormous doors were pushed open by guards—three to each door—and another four led the way in to ensure the way remained clear.

As they reached the dais, the guards split in two and took up posts at either side.

Finally, *finally*, Cimar appeared, dressed in full plate armor minus helmet and gauntlets, Leonine a couple of paces behind and dressed in equally fine mail, as full plate armor was only bestowed once spurs had been earned. Behind them came several men, towering and muscular, poles braced on their shoulders to carry the enormous lindworm skin secured with thick rope that had been woven into a makeshift net.

Despite the impressiveness of the skin, Davrin's eyes were only for Cimar, as beautiful as ever, though he definitely looked exhausted behind his façade of triumphant knight.

As they reached the dais, Cimar and Leonine knelt in perfect unison, hands splayed on the floor, heads bowed. "Your Majesty, I return from my quest triumphant, with trophy in hand to prove the veracity of my claim."

Behind him, the men carrying the lindworm skin set it to rest on the floor and knelt as well. At some point, the skin must have been properly treated, because it gleamed in the light of the countless torches in the hall, neatly rolled, with no hint of blood or other remnants of the beast to which it had once been attached.

"So I see," King Rorlen replied. "How did you manage such a feat on your own, Sir Cimar, when entire armies have been felled by a single lindworm?"

"It was asleep when we arrived, and my shifting ability gave me rare advantage." That set murmurs through the hall like waves. Anyone who hadn't been curious about Cimar's unknown shifted form before certainly was now. "I also suspect that until that point, it had never faced a foe who was a genuine threat, and so was ill-prepared. In short, Your Majesty, I managed the feat due almost entirely to luck."

Davrin sincerely doubted that, but Cimar wasn't a fool to go boasting and bragging, especially to the king barely tolerating this whole affair to begin with.

"Whatever the reason," King Rorlen said begrudgingly, "a victory is a victory, if it is fairly and honorably won. As you are the first to return victorious, I name you the winner of the quest challenge and award the full fifty points."

That meant even when Grayne completed his own quest, he could not earn more than forty points, even if he did exceedingly well. It wasn't much of a lead, especially as this was only the first of three, but it was something.

Applause filled the hall, bouncing off the walls and making the noise near-deafening.

When it finally quieted, Princess Korena said, "You went above and beyond in this matter, Sir Cimar. No one in history has bested a lindworm singlehandedly, not that anyone has recorded. It is my right to offer you a boon, and I do so. You may have what you wish, so long as it does not give you unfair advantage in the challenge or bring harm to others."

That earned Korena a glower from her father and sent whispers through the hall, but it was well within the rules. Moreover, the accomplishment was great enough King Rorlen himself should have granted a boon, and so could hardly argue when his own heir did so in his stead.

"My squire," Cimar replied, giving no sign of the stir all around him. "Whether I win or lose this challenge, he has already more than earned his spurs. He cannot be granted them during the challenge, of course, but at its conclusion, I would see him properly knighted. I would not have his honor or future besmirched by my actions, should the worst come to pass."

Korena smiled, faint but true, every bit the stately queen she would soon be as she replied, "The boon is granted, Sir Cimar. Pending formalities aside, congratulations on your knighthood, Sir Leonine."

"T-thank you, Your Highness," Leonine said, eyes wide before he hastily bowed his head again.

More whispers rippled through the hall but were cut off as Rorlen abruptly stood—and seemed for a moment to sway on his feet, regaining his balance right as it looked as though Grayne or nearby bodyguards would have to lunge to catch him. "Dismissed," Rorlen said, the word not quite spoken in a snarl, and strode off unsteadily, vanishing through the door that led to his private suite.

Davrin caught Cimar's eye and gestured for Cimar to come see him once he had a chance. Cimar nodded, and with a slight bow to Korena, Davrin slipped from the over-crowded hall and made his way back to his chamber.

CHAPTER SIX

Cimar had never been so sick of people in his life. By the time he managed to escape the onslaught of grabby hands and grossly inappropriate questions, and not-remotely-subtle attempts to glean his shifted form, he was ready to take up life as a hermit.

Or nearly, anyway. More than anything, he wanted to see Davrin, and finally say—and do—all those things he'd held back, for one reason or another, most of which seemed stupid now. He would have never dishonored his wife, but they'd come to their arrangement a long time ago.

If the lindworm had done nothing else, it had reminded him life was short, and nothing was worse than dying with important things left unsaid.

First, however, he released Leonine to go find his lovers, who would no doubt be delighted to console him over their grisly mission and congratulate him on his knighthood.

Second, he headed down to the armory, where the men he'd hired had already delivered the skin to the royal smiths. Cimar wasn't remotely surprised to find every last one of them clustered around the enormous skin taking up a goodly portion of their yard.

The chief blacksmith, and master of the armory, Croy, spied him first. "Didn't expect to see you before tomorrow, if not the day after. Was sure they'd keep you busy in that hall all night and day."

Cimar laughed. "They tried, but I would like rest, not so much wine I make myself sick. They are welcome to drink my share."

The blacksmiths all laughed, and then Croy motioned to the skin. "Know what you want to be done with it, or still deciding? There's enough here for several suits of plate and more besides. Could damn near outfit a small army." As master of the armory, Croy focused on making weapons when he wasn't simply keeping the place in order, but he'd apprenticed first in armor and could hold his own with any armorer in the place. "If we're talking weapons… you could outfit a few large armies."

"What in the world would I do with my own armies, other than make His Majesty think I'm plotting treason? No, thank you. Full plate for me, and again for my squire, to have when he's formally knighted. Swords and matching daggers as well. Two measures each for His Majesty and Her Highness. A dagger and full jewelry set for Lord Davrin, with opals. If there's anything left after that, I'll figure something out."

"There'll be plenty left," Croy said. "I'll keep you posted on the progress, and well done, Sir Cimar. May your name go down in history."

"May there be no more lindworms," Cimar replied, and departed, leaving the blacksmiths cheerfully arguing over the finer points of the new work they'd been given. For most of them, it would be their first time working with lindworm scales, but there would be damaged segments used for practice.

With that final duty executed, he returned to his chambers and had a couple of the guards stationed in the hall assist him with his armor. Someone, likely Davrin, had arranged for a bath to be waiting, for which Cimar was exceedingly grateful.

Roughly an hour or later, dressed in warm clothes that felt like nothing after days of wearing armor, heavy even when the weight was properly distributed. His soft boots, meant for walking around the castle, seemed weak and inefficient compared to the sturdy ones he'd worn into the mountains.

He knocked on Davrin's door and nearly jumped when it was opened as he'd barely finished. Davrin smiled. "You could have waited until morning, but I'm glad you came." He stepped back and let Cimar inside, closing the door quietly behind him.

A lot of things washed over Cimar at once: that as careful and contained as Davrin was, it was clear he was on edge about something; food had been laid out, more than enough for two; there was a ring on Davrin's on left hand that hadn't been there before, and it bore a hawk's eye stone; a duplicate of the ring and what looked like a royal ring of state were strung on a chain around his neck, clearly so Cimar would see them.

"What is going on?"

"A lot," Davrin replied. "You were gone mere days, but that was more than enough time for... well, everything to change. I have leave from Her Highness to discuss all of it with you, but how about you eat and relax first? I'm sure you'd like to be off your feet for a bit and simply doing nothing."

What Cimar wanted to do was kiss the man breathless and figure out the rest of the evening from there, but as tempting as that was, he would *try* to act like a reasonable adult with some sense of honor and decorum. So he settled for smiling. "That would be nice, I concede. Thank you for doing all this."

"All I did was ask it be done," Davrin said dryly. "I'm a noble. The only work we do is talk endlessly about how everyone else should go about solving problems."

Cimar laughed as he took the seat Davrin indicated. "I think you do a bit more than that."

"Write a lot of letters."

Still chuckling, Cimar poured wine for them both from the pitcher in the middle of the table and filled his plate with a bit of everything: veal tart, gravé of birds, which was a favorite chicken dish of his, fennel sausages, fresh bread, onion tart, cheese, stuffed eggs, and chopped spinach and artichokes. It was, quite literally, a feast fit for a king. "How did you convince the kitchens to bring all this up here?"

"I would love to say it's because they like me, but the truth is that they were eager to do something for the mighty Sir Cimar, Noble Champion and Lindworm Slayer."

Cimar sighed. "I suppose that is what will follow me the rest of my life now."

"You have to concede it's quite the achievement. Even the great Sir Bermont, the Black Dragon, did not achieve anything half so great."

"Sir Bermont was a drunken wastrel who took credit for the work his army did," Cimar replied. "I've read the personal accounts of many of them, and he does not deserve the legends that keep his name alive."

Davrin snickered. "Nothing like reading to disillusion one of… well, practically everything."

They settled into an easy silence after that, enjoying the food and quiet. Eventually, though, Cimar's curiosity would no longer be contained. "All right, my patience is at an end. How, in the few days I was gone, did you come to join the Order of the Osprey?"

"I've 'joined' quite a bit more than that,"

Davrin replied, setting aside his knife and fork, finishing his wine and cleaning his mouth and hands before settling back in his chair with a far more solemn mien than Cimar had expected. "I'm engaged to Her Highness." Before Cimar could find word to reply to that, too distracted by the shattering of his heart and fragile hopes, Davrin explained all that had transpired in his absence.

As he finished, he stood and removed the chain from around his neck and slid the second Osprey ring free. "She bid me give this to you, and said that you have more than earned it simply by rising to the challenge."

Cimar rose as Davrin came around the table and offered the ring. Accepting it, Cimar slid the ring into place on his own left hand. "Thank you. Congratulations, as well, on your pending marriage. You'll make an excellent prince consort." He smiled, hoping none of his sadness showed. At least he'd found out before he'd gone and made a perfect fool of himself. "I should—"

"I'm not finished," Davrin cut in, drawing himself up slightly, and that impression of being on edge returned, stronger than ever, commanding Cimar's full attention. "There was something else Her Highness discussed with me this afternoon. She wanted me to know that Lady Aliara is her lover, has been for some time, and she had no intention of severing that relationship. So naturally, she added, she would never expect me to end my love affair with you, so long as I was willing to do my duty in providing heirs."

"End your—" Cimar stopped. Opened his mouth. Closed it. "She thinks we're lovers? What did you say?"

Davrin offered a wispy smile, like amusement wanted out, but a fit of nerves would not let it. So unusual in a man who had made a life's practice of arguing with monarchs on behalf of his own king. A man who would soon be practically a king himself. "I told her we weren't lovers, because so many things made it impossible, but that I'd always wished that wasn't true."

Cimar's head spun with all the revelations striking him. Somehow, fighting the lindworm was seeming like the simplest, easiest part of his week. All the shattered pieces in his chest started to slowly, tentatively draw back together. "You did? I mean, you do? Whatever, come here." He reached out, snagged Davrin's tunic in both hands, and reeled him in close and kissed the bloody fool even as Davrin gasped his name in surprise.

It took only a moment for Davrin to catch up and meet him full measure. His arms, far stronger than Cimar would have expected, wrapped firmly around Cimar's waist and lifted him slightly, so they were more of a level in height. That made Cimar's grip awkward, so he gladly shifted to sink his hands into Davrin's hair, which was even softer than it had always looked.

His mouth was soft too, warm and still flavored of their dinner, but the kiss itself was ardent, focused, sending delicate shivers down Cimar's spine as he imagined all the other delightful things that mouth and tongue could do.

When they finally drew apart, he was panting. He stared as Davrin slowly let him slide down so his feet were on the floor again. "How long have you…"

Davrin's smile was bittersweet. "I said always, and I meant it. There just constantly seemed to be obstacles that could not be overcome, bridges that could not be crossed."

"Yes, speaking of obstacles, I am still very much married, and that will not look good for you," Cimar replied. He'd given up caring a long time ago how it made *him* look, but he wouldn't have his besmirched reputation harming Davrin.

"Korena said she would see that taken care of, and made it quite clear I was to take care of the rest." He curled a finger beneath Cimar's chin, tilting his head up just that bit farther, and mercy of the Goddess, Cimar would never survive if Davrin was now going to make a habit of looking at him like that.

He licked his lip, enjoying far too much the effect that had, the strangled noise Davrin made. "Then get on with it, my lord, and take care of the rest." He grinned. "Unless, of course, the diplomat in you requires more dithering."

Davrin grabbed hold and shuffled him

toward the bed, moving so fast that, forced to stumble backward, Cimar would have fallen if not for Davrin's secure grip. Then he was sprawled awkwardly on the bed, legs dangling over the edge, completely uncaring as all his attention focused on Davrin. "Diplomats never dither. We simply know when and how to take our time."

Cimar groaned, fit to burst as that hot promise coursed through him, better even than the rush of flame when he was a dragon. "I admit I had hopes and ambitions upon my return, but I also confess I did not think I would enjoy such rousing success." He sat up and set to work on his clothes, resenting all the layers required to endure the bitter cold.

As they both finished undressing, leaving their clothes in heaps they'd likely regret later, Davrin climbed into the bed and drew the curtains, cocooning them in darkness, but also warmth. Firelight slipped through cracks in the curtains, just enough for him to see by as Davrin settled between his thighs. Cimar shuddered, nearly undone right then and there. "I like having you there, my lord. Or should I say, my prince?"

"I'd rather hear something far more possessive," Davrin replied, and took his mouth in a kiss that left their first one in the dust, tasting every corner and crevice of his mouth, sucking on his tongue, biting at his lips until they were pleasantly sore and swollen from all the attention.

Shifting away from Cimar's mouth, Davrin

put his own to work on the rest of Cimar, starting at his jaw and working his way slowly—agonizingly slowly—down his body, alternating between lips and teeth and tongue, leaving a trail of kisses, licks, and teasing nips that Cimar would feel whenever he closed his eyes or simply let his mind wander.

Every time he tried to do some touching of his own, all he got for his efforts were his hands pushed back to the bedding, until he gave up and did as told, more than happy to be at Davrin's mercy if that was what he desired.

Davrin bit sharply at one hip, right above bone, making Cimar gasp and arch, a weakness even he hadn't known was there to exploit. Soft chuckles filled their private little world, and Davrin did it again, forcing Cimar to slap a hand over his mouth lest he make a noise that the guards in the hall would hear all too clearly.

By the time Davrin's teeth grazed along the inner skin of his thighs, he was gasping and pleading and taking the Goddess's name quite vigorously in vain. When Davrin's mouth finally, *finally* dropped over his cock, Cimar didn't know whether to sob or scream, and wound up doing some utterly ridiculous combination of the two that he had to muffle with a pillow.

The bastard had not been lying about taking his time; Cimar didn't know whether to kiss him for it later or kill him.

Deft fingers toyed with his sack, stroking

and gently tugging, rolling his balls in a way equal parts amazing and agonizing. All the while Davrin sucked at his cock, taking him deep, into his throat, tongue working the underside, cheeks hollowed. His jaw must have been aching by that point, but he only continued on. Releasing Cimar's sack, Davrin reached further back with his free hand and teased at Cimar's hole, pressing a fingertip in the barest bit, and that was the last that Cimar could take. The hitching of his breath was all the warning he could manage before he gripped Davrin's beautiful, mussed hair and spilled down his throat, ragged cries filling the air, Cimar far too overtaken to remember to muffle them this time. Well, the guards would have something other than the lindworm to talk about, for better or worse.

Chest heaving, he collapsed fully on the bed, sweaty and overheated and more enthralled than ever with the beautiful man still braced above him. Sweat gleamed on Davrin's skin in the bare bits of light that reached them, and his mouth was a mess of spittle and come, his hair a hopeless tangle as it spilled over his shoulders. Cimar had never seen a more beautiful sight. He reached up and tugged Davrin down, kissed him deeply, groaning at the taste of himself in Davrin's mouth, shivers running through him despite the fact he was far too wrung out to do much of anything the rest of the night.

Although there was definitely one thing he

had the energy for, though the details he'd leave up to Davrin. To his lover. Cimar wanted to laugh, the joy was so consuming. Drawing back, biting playfully at Davrin's well-used lips, he said, "I'm starting to suspect your diplomatic methods, my prince."

"I've had offers," Davrin said, and Cimar could all but feel him rolling his eyes. "None appealed enough to drag myself into the mess such methods cause."

"What about my offers? Would you find those appealing?"

Davrin bit at his throat, right below his collarbone, and Cimar could feel how much he already appealed from the hard cock pressing against him, leaving warm, sticky trails on his skin. "Perhaps."

"You want my mouth or my ass?" Cimar asked, the words coming out a touch breathlessly. That got him a positively delightful noise, like Davrin was so desperately overcome, everything jumbled together into a wordless heap wholly unlike a man whose life was built around using his words with more skill than most.

After a moment, Davrin managed raggedly, "I want to fuck you."

"Then get on with it, my prince."

Davrin laughed, the sound edged with tension and desperation, and then he was moving away to retrieve something from one of the little cabinets that occupied the head of the bed, and which Cimar had definitely not noticed until that moment. "On your knees, champion mine."

Hopefully, they'd soon get a chance to do this in daylight, where he could insist upon remaining on his back so he could see Davrin's face when he came. For the moment, though, Cimar was more than happy to comply, turning and settling on his hands and knees, spreading wide so Davrin had plenty of room.

Davrin's fingers were as talented as his mouth, and Cimar's spent cock did its level best to rise again as Davrin worked him open, twisting and stretching, knowing exactly how to crook those fingers to make him groan and beg, until Davrin at last replaced those fingers with his cock.

He slid in slowly at first, but just as Cimar was seriously considering murder, Davrin pulled out and thrust back in hard, knocking the thought and the breath right out of him, doing it again before Cimar could even think to recover. Davrin set a pace that had Cimar clutching first at the bedding, and then bracing himself against the elaborate headboard. Sweat stung his eyes, and his lungs were going to give out, but it would be worth the steep price. He rocked in time with Davrin's pounding thrusts, meeting them as best he could but mostly just trying to hold steady.

A second climax took him so hard and sudden he felt dizzy. The hands on his hips tightened, and Davrin sank into him one last time, plastering himself against Cimar's back as he came, breath hot on his skin.

They collapsed in a sweaty, panting pile, and Cimar whimpered when Davrin gently pulled out of him. Exhaustion fell over him like a blanket, the long, arduous day and its unexpectedly delightful end finally taking their toll, and the last thing he remembered was a soft kiss to his lips.

~~*

He woke to darkness and the muffled sounds of a roaring fire. He also woke alone, which was disappointing, but as he listened, he could hear the soft, dry crackle of turning pages. Yawning, he pushed through the curtains and out of the bed, immediately shivering in the cold, drawing the attention of the handsome figure by the fire.

Davrin closed his book and set it aside. "You should have stayed in bed." He stood and crossed to Cimar, pulling him in close, wrapping him in warmth and the scent of woodsmoke and brandy, and faded hints of sex.

"I admit I didn't think things through; I simply wanted to see you."

Davrin chuckled and discarded the heavy bed robe he'd been wearing before getting them both back into the warm bed, drawing the curtains closed. "I woke a short time ago and couldn't go back to sleep. Too many thoughts."

"You knocked the thoughts right out of me," Cimar said, settling alongside him, head on Davrin's chest. His heart beat rapidly in his chest; he'd imagined this very scenario a thousand times or more, but never once thought it would come to pass. "I'm still not convinced this isn't some dying dream, and the lindworm got me after all."

"Don't say such horrible things," Davrin replied. "I'm no less stunned, believe me. I accepted a long time ago that I would never be able to call you my lover. I was honored enough to count you a friend, and humbled you agreed to be my champion. I feel greedy and spoiled, but I'm not inclined to give you up, either."

Cimar kissed his chest, then shifted and leaned up to drop another on his mouth. "The path you took led you here, and it seems to me here is a fine place to be, Your Highness. Good for you, good for many, especially after all the damage His Majesty has done. Princess Korena will have her work cut out for her, regaining the trust of the people, rebuilding foreign relations her father has shattered or let waste from neglect. She's smart and clever to take you as her consort." He laughed as fanciful images flitted through his head. "Not to mention the children will be adorable and grow to be beautiful adults."

"It doesn't bother you?"

"What?"

"That she and I will have intimate relations, probably many times."

Cimar sighed. "If we had done this as youths, if I'd never married and one of us had worked up the nerve to approach the other? Perhaps. But I did marry, and Rosa and I... well, we learned quickly that while we were good friends, we did not do well living together as husband and wife. We tried anyway, because that's what you're supposed to do. Marry, make the best of the situation, no matter how bad that situation might be. Ours was certainly not the worst—no abuse, no neglect, nothing like that. We simply had different wants and needs, and finally we sat down one night and simply *talked*. Decided we should do what was best for *us*, even if that meant going against convention.

"So that's what we did. We lived as friends. Had lovers. Different lives. Rosa met her farmer, who already had three children, one of them a mere babe. We talked again, and even after the king refused to negate our marriage, she left to be with him, with my blessing. I've never seen her happier. My squire is in love with a married couple, and I suspect they might return those affections. A great many people I know, in fact, are happier because they realized that rules are only as unbreakable as we want them to be. They're a cage made of smoke, and I've never missed finally letting that smoke drift away. What matters is if the four of us are all right with our unconventional arrangement, and it sounds to me like we are."

Cimar kissed him again, chuckling as he drew back. "Anyway, only a person with no sexual interest whatsoever would look at Her Highness and feel nothing. We should all be made to suffer such a duty as that."

"Knave," Davrin replied, and drew Cimar into a kiss that promised they'd soon both be so exhausted they'd likely sleep until noon.

CHAPTER SEVEN

Grayne finished his quest in desultory fashion, as though it was a chore he was accustomed to fobbing off on servants. That probably wasn't entirely untrue. At best he should have been awarded twenty points, and that was generous.

King Rorlen gave him thirty-five, and Davrin was fairly certain that was only because Korena managed to get through his head how bad it would look if he awarded the full forty.

As the day dawned on the Royal Frost Fair, a long tradition for celebrating the winter solstice, the count stood at fifty to thirty-five, and the great Lindworm Slayer greatly favored. King Rorlen was not remotely amused by the situation, but there was little he could do about it overtly.

Covertly, however, was another matter entirely. He'd already ensured Grayne had only to overcome a gap of fifteen points. Next would be the endurance challenge, and he would be certain to give Grayne every advantage he could.

Davrin's heart believed Cimar could overcome any challenge. His mind, however, honed by years of royal histrionics and courtly scheming, was grimly certain that Cimar would not come out the winner this day.

He dressed with care, even more so than usual, donning a tunic of deep blue that had been embroidered with scattered rowan leaves in icy blue and silvery white, so they looked frosted. It was pure chance the embroidery was rowan leaves, but it worked out far too nicely for him not to put it to full use.

When his hair was up and he'd donned a cloak sure to keep him warm for all the hours he'd be outside, Davrin headed off.

The fair was always held in an enormous field a few minutes' ride from the royal castle, where once drills and tournaments and more had taken place, all focused on honing soldiers for war. Thankfully, such measures were not as required, and the soldiers had long since moved elsewhere, to a place far more suited to their reduced needs.

The weather was absolutely perfect: snow falling gently, but not so heavily that it would cause significant interference. It was cold, of course, but not unbearably so, and already the hot beer and mulled wine were flowing, along with all manner of street food that set Davrin's stomach to rumbling. As hungry as he was, though, food would have to wait until after the opening ceremonies.

As he reached the area where they would

take place, he wasn't surprised to see one of Korena's private servants waiting for him. The woman greeted him and bid him follow her to the royal box.

That was significantly more a statement than requesting he join her for dinner. Something must be wrong, that she would show such flagrant favoritism—or she expected something was going to go wrong.

He bowed low to King Rorlen, who dismissed him with a grunt and barely a glance. Moving on, Davrin bowed to Korena, making certain this one was just a touch deeper, a touch longer. She smiled softly and offered her hand, letting it linger when he kissed the back of it. "Good morning, Lord Dweller-by-the-Sea."

"Good morning, Your Highness. You are looking more beautiful than ever. Lady Aliara, an honor, as ever."

"Lord Dweller-by-the-Sea," she greeted. "I wish you and your champion victory on the field today."

"Thank you."

He sat as Korena motioned him to the chair on her left, where he would sit as prince consort. "You're making interesting decisions this morning."

"My father had another fit last night."

"I see."

"We are carrying on, but I'm increasingly worried."

"Whatever you need or want, I will serve, my queen."

She smiled, genuine and open. "Thank you, my lord. Truly I do look forward to calling you my husband."

"It will be the greatest honor of my life."

Her smile turned mischievous. "From what I'm hearing about where Sir Cimar slept last night, I think he might take issue with being second place."

Davrin burst out laughing, drawing a few looks from several nearby individuals. More quietly, so the words wouldn't carry, he replied, "Sir Cimar knows full well where he stands with me."

"I'm glad."

A servant came up requiring Korena's attention, and Davrin left her to her duties, content to watch the milling crowd slowly filling the seats surrounding the field. He would have loved to be able to walk in with Cimar, noble and champion together, friends and now lovers. As the next part of the challenge was to take place right after the opening ceremonies, though, Cimar had preparations to make.

Nearly another hour or so passed before the king signaled the waiting trumpeters, who immediately played the signal to start. An excited hush rippled through the crowd, and as King Rorlen stood, Davrin rose with everyone else, offering his arm as he escorted Korena to the edge of the royal box. She waved to everyone as her father started speaking, causing a brief disruption as everyone cheered for her.

King Rorlen gave roughly the same speech every year, modified in small ways to remain relevant. It was not hard to tell that everyone knew the speech by heart, had no interest in the perfunctory changes.

The crowd did not stir until the trumpets sounded again, this time heralding the arrival of knights. Grayne and Cimar entered the ring from a wide archway. As always, Cimar was resplendent, the very image of a knight, like he could have stepped from a painting or a tapestry. Next to him, Grayne had finally made some effort, but he was still a pale, pathetic shadow of Cimar.

They knelt several paces away from the royal box, one hand splayed for balance, the other across their chests, heads bowed.

"Knights, good morning and welcome to the second part of your challenge. Today will be a test of endurance. You are to report to the south side of Queen Tane Lake, where you will be expected to swim all the way across to us here at the north side."

Cimar's face gave nothing away, but Grayne radiated smugness. It was not hard to see how it would all play out. King Rorlen might be going insane, but that didn't equate to stupid.

Dismissing the knights, King Rorlen called for the festivities to begin, and the crowds erupted into cheers before they began the usual mad dash to go off to find good seats for their favorite events, or to be first in line for various foods, prize giveaways, and more.

He had a feeling most of the crowd was heading straight for the northern shore of the lake.

Offering his arm to Korena again, he walked with her to the lake. "Was this your father's idea?"

"I suspect it was Tekker's, however against the rules that might be. I am sorry. Sir Cimar is the finest knight I know, but given Grayne's abilities and how flagrantly he'll use them today, it's clear he will take the victory points."

Davrin lifted one shoulder. "It's fine. Hardly surprising that after the shocking beginning of a lindworm, His Majesty would seek to even the odds—make them dead even, in fact."

Korena looked at him, brows shooting up. "You think he's going to ensure they end this test tied for points?" Her brow furrowed then. It was rather adorable, the up, down, up, down. "Yes, I see what you mean. Shrewd, very shrewd. Definitely Tekker's doing. My father would prefer to give an easy victory and be done with the matter, not drag it out and add dramatics like this." She sighed.

"Dramatics garner support. Nobody loves a boring, efficient meeting. Everybody loves when that meeting is disrupted by the Ambassador of Wallow losing his temper and dropping Crown

Prince Tarsenya with a single punch."

Laughing, Korena replied, "I admit I would pay good money to have seen that. Tarsenya could use more drop-punches."

"He's smug and obnoxious, I grant you that, but he's shrewd and oddly direct for a diplomat. I've dealt with far worse."

Korena smiled, and they fell silent as they joined the milling crowd, who were kept at bay by bodyguards, but only somewhat, as Korena disliked being as removed and 'locked away' as her father.

They took their places on the royal dais when they reached the lake.

It was named for the tragic queen who'd killed herself there after a lifetime of tragedies, one piled right on top of the other, like the central figure in the world's most depressing play. They'd found her body in the morning, floating in the middle of the lake where the weights she'd improvised had failed to keep her at the bottom as she'd wished.

Davrin could not decide if it was the worst possible place to hold a challenge for a man wrongfully murdered, or if it was all too apropos.

All he hoped was that Cimar would be all right. The lake was cold in the middle of summer; in the midst of winter it was not just brutal, but fatal. Only those with magic, be they shifters or otherwise, stood any sort of chance of making such a treacherous journey. That was just the cold.

The lake itself was enormous, large enough that nearly a hundred royal castles could fit into it easily.

They would not be swimming the widest part of it, but the designated area was wide enough, especially with the frigid temperature piled on top. It wasn't just a test of endurance: it was practically murder.

The worst part of being a spectator was, as with so many things in life, the waiting. The lake was too wide, even at this relatively small stretch, for them to see Cimar and Grayne for much of the swim.

It was not remotely reassuring that some poor group of servants had been forced to come out well before the test and break up a great deal of the ice. Even now they were out there ensuring the way remained clear.

If Davrin had not possessed years of training in dealing with such terrors and frustrations, he might have lost his temper—and common sense—and punched King Rorlen right in the face. Challenges were supposed to be dangerous, but they weren't meant to be promises of certain death.

The cry went out, and from across the lake he could just barely hear the ringing of the gong to signal Cimar and Grayne to start.

He was immensely grateful right then that his ties to Princess Korena meant he got a prize position at the lakeshore.

It took less time than he thought to see effects of the race, and he wasn't surprised by what they saw: steam.

A few minutes later, what he'd been dreading came into view: Grayne, in his shifted form, swimming at a speed he'd never achieve as a human, and his hellhound form so hot that he was all but impervious to the cold.

Contrary to their name, hellhounds were only dogs in the barest sense of that word. They were more like wolves, for one, but far more than that, they were somewhere in between human and wolf. Longer than usual legs and arms, covered head to toe in fur that was mostly black but turned into reds and oranges at the extremities, like burned wood tipped in remaining flame. Up close, his eyes would be like glowing coals, and he radiated so much heat that no one could stand closer than twenty paces or so.

It should have been declared cheating, but no one could say that now, because Cimar had won his first challenge by way of his shifted form. He'd had good reason, but it set a precedent that Grayne was now going to flagrantly abuse.

Grayne reached the shore minutes later, heaving himself up and out in a cloud of steam, leaving a trail of hot water and dead fish behind him. Next to Davrin, Korena's mouth was pinched tight, and she only looked angrier as her father loudly and enthusiastically declared Grayne the winner and awarded the full fifty points.

They waited several more minutes, long and agonizing, before Cimar finally appeared. He was moving much more slowly, clearly hating every moment and struggling greatly, but he *was* managing it. He must be using magic in some way; otherwise he'd be dead, no matter how amazing he was.

As Cimar reached the shore, he managed to wade—and then crawl—out of the water on his own. The moment he was clear of it, and the challenge officially over, Davrin surged forward and dried Cimar off himself, taking one of the drying cloths right from Leonine with a hasty apology. When he was dry, Davrin wrapped Cimar in his own cloak.

A healer came up then and pressed a hand to Cimar chest, murmuring softly. Light flowed from her hand, and then over Cimar, and a few moments later his shivering eased, the magic warming him from the core outward in a way nothing else could.

"You going to be all right?" Davrin asked, combing damp strands of hair from his face. He knew damn well the rumors that would fly now, but for once in his life he simply did not care. Cimar not dying because of the unreasonable demands of a petulant king was all that concerned him.

Cimar bobbed his head. "I'm fine. Miserable, but fine. The more time passes, the better I'll be. I am sorry I could not win this one, my lord."

"You've no reason to be sorry for being the victim of petty machinations. *Deadly* machinations, at that. Come on, let's get you some mulled wine and food to replenish your strength."

As he spoke, though, servants came up bearing said wine and food, and Leonine with his clothes. Even His Majesty did not demand that Cimar first attend him, but waited until he'd recovered from the ordeal.

When Cimar finally did kneel before King Rorlen, Davrin could see he was not the only one who was unsurprised when Cimar was awarded thirty-five points for his performance in the challenge.

Eighty-five to Eighty-five. Victory rested entirely on the final test. Cimar stood no chance of victory against a hellhound unless he had a shifted form that was stronger and which he was willing to use.

He'd been backed into a corner, one way or another.

Davrin was sick to his stomach. He'd never wanted this—the man he loved forced to fight for his life against monsters, freezing cold, and a cheating bastard who fought like a rabid wolf. This should have been a fair challenge. There was no strategic reason to turn it into this debacle.

After the crowds had dispersed, and the people who'd wanted to speak personally to him and Cimar—most to congratulate Cimar on how well he'd done, all things considered, but some trying to sniff out what was going on between Davrin and Her Highness—had left, Davrin smiled. "I'm sure you're long past tired of the attention, but truly you're magnificent, Cimar."

Cimar's mouth ticked up at one corner. The exhaustion poured from his every crack and crevice, but his smile was true as he replied, "You can show me how magnificent after I've had some rest."

Happiness and excitement ran through Davrin, banishing the cold that had crept in while he'd stood without his cloak. In all the distractions, he'd completely forgotten that one tiny detail: he could flirt with Cimar now. "That was a given."

Smile widening, Cimar motioned they should depart. "I saw you were with Her Highness. Is she making more of a show now? Is that wise? I assume so, given the two of you have an acumen for politics that I will never possess."

"Well, I certainly do not possess your impressive skillset. She is making more of a show, yes. I think she is starting to hint to people the way things are going to go, or at least could go. One should always be careful about displeasing their king, but it would also be treacherous to displease their future queen, especially when it's becoming painfully clear she will assume the throne in the very near future. Allegiances are shifting; always a dangerous time in court."

Worry cut into Cimar's face. "How dangerous is it for you?"

"Because of my new arrangement?" When Cimar nodded, Davrin replied, "At present, the danger is minimal to non-existent. My greatest threat right now is the challenge, and they're taking it out on you. Speaking of, I hope you'll be all right in the duel. I have every faith in you, but I also have every faith Trekker is a conniving bastard and Grayne an inveterate cheater."

Cimar laughed. "Grayne bested me today, but I always knew he would win the endurance challenge. I can take him in a duel."

"I apologize for all the attention this has brought you, especially the invasions of your privacy. I know you especially like to keep your shifted form private, and the duel stands a good chance of violating that."

"I entered knowing full well what could happen, please don't apologize." Cimar leaned in, as if about to kiss him, and stilled himself just in time. "Sorry. Do cease to fret and worry and feel guilty, though, please?"

Davrin smiled and nodded slightly. "I shall do my best, I vow it. Later, though, I want that kiss."

"You shall have it, and more besides."

"Come, let's go do something that gives you a chance to rest a bit." He led the way through the milling crowd, stopping occasionally to speak with someone, but mostly nodding to people and simply moving on.

They finally stopped at an improvised theatre to enjoy a play, and Davrin wasn't remotely surprised that Cimar fell asleep only minutes into it, even with the ruckus of the crowd. He left him to his rest throughout the play, and even as the crowd dispersed once it was over. Only then did he reluctantly shake Cimar awake.

Yawning, Cimar said, "Did I fall asleep? Some champion I am."

"Yes, horrible champion, killing a lindworm and swimming across a frozen lake. You should be ashamed."

Cimar laughed. "Come on, I'm hungry again. Thank you for the rest. I'm sure I must have amused quite a few people, snoring away through a noisy play in the middle of the frost fair."

"I'm pretty sure there were a few others in the crowd doing the same thing, and they were the ones snoring, not you."

"Well, that's something."

Davrin rose and offered a hand to Cimar, pulling him to his feet, hating he could not simply take a kiss right then and there. Eventually, when matters had quieted down, when the marriage and shifts of power were settled into place, he'd be able to. If his own wife did not complain about his lover, the rest of the world could hardly say a word. "What would you like to do?"

"I would not be opposed to more food, and maybe a walk in the quiet when we're done, to work off the food and…" Cimar winked. "Clear my head."

"I don't know why I thought you would be the less bold of the two of us."

Cimar laughed. "Neither do I. You've literally been trained not to be bold, and knights often rely on bold measures, though it's a fine line between bold and reckless."

"Like single-handedly killing a lindworm."

"Yes, like that," Cimar said with a sigh.

They stopped at a couple of food stalls, loading up on pies and other treats that could be eaten as they walked. By the time they cleared the fairgrounds, food devoured, Davrin was ready for a nap himself. Snow was still softly falling, though, and it was hard to do anything but focus wholly on the man beside him, who looked like a winter prince snuck away from his immortal realm to play amongst mortals.

"I do not know what thoughts fill your head, but I rather like them. They look like the kind of thoughts that lead to hiding in the trees for kisses."

Davrin smiled and went easily as Cimar pulled him in amongst the aforementioned trees and pushed him gently up against the trunk of a particularly large one. He tasted like quail pie and mulled wine, his hands quite sure of themselves as they sank into Davrin's hair to keep his head right where Cimar wanted it.

Far be it for him to complain.

CHAPTER EIGHT

Three days later, Cimar still could not go anywhere about the castle or city without someone stopping him to discuss the lindworm, the challenge in general, or attempt to get information out of him regarding Davrin and Her Highness.

He was sick of it, but there was nothing to be done save get used to it. He was going to be the champion of a prince consort—his life would never entirely be his again. It was intimidating and exhausting, but he'd surrender far more than his solitary, quiet life to stand by Davrin's side the way he'd always wanted.

Cimar took a seat on a bench outside a temple and sighed, grateful to be off his feet for a time, and in no rush to return to the castle and frost fair, for all he was looking forward to having the matter over and done with.

Lee had wanted to come with him, but Cimar preferred him as far from the drama as possible. He wouldn't put it past Grayne or Tekker to use Lee against him—hurt him, even kill him, whatever it took to make Cimar falter or break long enough they could land the final victory.

If they did hurt Lee, nothing and no one would stop Cimar from stopping them for good.

He scrubbed at his face, longing for a place he could curl up and sleep undisturbed for several hours. Or where he could hide away with Davrin for several hours and do far more delightful things undisturbed.

That brought a smile to his face and improved his mood slightly. If there was one thing he'd not expected to come from this challenge, it was the romance of his impossible dreams.

What would Ballior say if he could see all that had come about because of his death? More than likely he'd simply laugh and say or do something to really set off Tekker and Grayne. Those two generally didn't care enough about anyone to muster something as strong as hate, but they'd hated Ballior and all the thousand ways he'd thwarted them over the years.

Cimar would be damned if they got away with murdering him.

He might be damned anyway, for thinking such vengeful thoughts unbecoming a knight, but he didn't care. Justice would be served for once.

Thankfully, he had a future queen and prince consort on his side.

Shaking his head at his meandering thoughts, he slowly stood, stretched out stiff muscles, and continued on to where his horse waited.

He'd only just reached it when he heard someone call his name in a frantic, frightened tone. Lee.

Cimar whipped around just as Lee came barreling to a stop right in front of him, mere steps short of crashing into him. "Lee?"

"Sir Cimar! You have to come at once, please, I think they're being threatened. They—" His voice broke then, and it seemed for a moment like tears might get the better of him. Which was so unlike Lee, it was nearly frightening.

Cimar grasped his shoulders and gave him a gentle shake, then pulled him into a tight embrace. "Lee, whatever is wrong, we will fix it. Calm down, now, all right? It's not like you to panic. You didn't act like this when we faced a *lindworm*, for love of the gods. All right there? Good. Now tell me what's wrong."

"I went to Everard and Odilia today, tell them what's been happening, invite them to my formal knighting…" Sorrow and pain filled his face. "They refuse to see me. Wouldn't even tell me to go away themselves, just had their bartender do it. Told me it was over, I needn't bother coming by anymore. Nothing I didn't—" He stopped, drew a shuddery breath. "Didn't expect to hear eventually, but it's not like them to speak through others. I left, but after a bit went back, just to settle my nerves, you know? Figure out if something was really wrong, or if I was just having a hard time dealing with 'no.' I was just about to give up when some men showed up. Thugs of some sort, cheap clothes but good armor and weapons. I swear I heard one of them complaining about Grayne. I just don't know to what purpose. Why bother them over a matter that doesn't really have anything to do with me? I'm just your squire."

"You're not 'just' anything, Lee," Cimar said quietly. "You're important to me, and that means you're of use to them. I am curious why they decided to harass your lovers, to what end they are working. Come on, let's go see if we can find answers before your Everard and Odilia come to further harm. Are they still at their inn?"

"They haven't left it today, so far as I can tell, even though this is usually when Odilia runs her weekly errands."

Cimar gave his horse the apple he'd bought for her and a brief pat before heading off once more. At least he didn't have to worry about his purchases; he'd had them all sent on to the castle so he wouldn't have to carry them around the city.

Thankfully, the Gold Cock wasn't far. "How did you know where to find me? You left before I did."

"I saw you when I was wandering around feeling sorry for myself, before I decided to go back and watch things, see if I really was just being petulant or if my gut was right and something was wrong."

"I'm glad you listened to your gut. I told you that you had flawless instincts."

"That's why I went back," Lee replied with a small smile. It collapsed in the next moment, though. "I hope they're all right. I just don't understand…"

Cimar pursed his lips. "It's certainly not the method I thought they would employ. Grayne must realize that his chances of winning the duel are minimal, even with cheating."

Lee smirked at that. "Poor Hellhound, worried he might not be the baddest beast at the ball."

"Oh, shush, you," Cimar said with a laugh.

The levity faded as they neared the street corner where the inn was located.

On the surface, nothing was amiss, but something nagged at him, something that snagged his subconscious but hadn't quite reached his conscious mind yet. "Where were you watching them?"

"Here," Lee said, and rolled his head to one side, signaling Cimar to follow him. They ducked into a narrow ally that smelled of piss, shit, and things Cimar preferred not to think about. "You're definitely cleaning my boots later."

Lee heaved a sigh. "Like I didn't already know that. Come on." He scaled a wall at the back, the uneven brickwork making it a relatively easy task.

From the roof of a house that was leaning

heavily into its neighbor, they had an excellent view of the inn and everybody who came and went. Up high, able to see the whole inn without the interference of the busy streets, Cimar could finally pick out what had been bothering him before.

Mercenaries, six of them. All dressed to look unremarkable, no obvious weapons in sight, but he knew soldiers when he saw them. "Mercenaries, at least six outside, probably the same inside, if not more. They're prepared for a fight, but why? Did they think you'd force your way in there to confront your lovers? What are we missing? Something isn't adding up. Would these mercenaries know what you look like?"

"I don't know. I doubt it, though. I recognize most of the local sword-hires, and these guys all look to be from out of town." Lee said. "I also tend to come and go pretty quietly, minimize the rumors that are stirred up. There are a handful of people that would recognize me as a regular, but not really more than that."

"I see. So… if you'd shown up to see them, and the only person you really saw or spoke to was the bartender, and *he* gave no indication of who you were, these guys would never know their target had come and gone. Does that sound feasible?"

Lee's eyes widened as the ramifications struck him. "They sent me away to protect me. They're still in danger."

"That's what I'm thinking."

"Damn it, I'm stupid for—"

"Not having the experience to think of such a scheme," Cimar interrupted. "Don't punish yourself for things you didn't do. You had the sense to come to me for help, Lee, and now you'll know what to look for should this, gods forbid, happen again. Come on, let's go save your lovers."

"What are we going to do?"

"Normally I'd suggest a quiet approach to get the lay of things, see if we couldn't sneak them out quietly. I don't think that will work here, unfortunately. They'll recognize me, if only by reputation, and by now they must realize something is amiss that you haven't arrived yet when you clearly were expected."

Lee perked up at that. "So we go in swinging."

"Yes. Reckless, but I think in this case it'll give us an advantage. They're braced for something quiet, the way they're spread out. They don't know who they're looking for, but they think it'll be a single person showing up for an afternoon tryst. Not a pair of soldiers. Come on, then. Just keep a couple of them alive so we have proof it's Tekker behind this."

"Understood."

They retraced their steps to the alley entrance. "We'll be facing at least twelve, but I'd assume twenty," Cimar said. "Our best chance is to surprise the group out front and take them out quickly, then deal with the remainder as they come out of the inn. We'll need your particular skillset to pull this off. Are you up for it?"

"Yes," Lee said.

"You take the left, I'll take the right. Once we've cleared the yard, focus on the stable entrance, and I'll focus on the main door."

Lee nodded and made certain his sword could be easily drawn, then flexed his fingers, sparks of rainbow light catching at the tips briefly.

Cimar loosened his sword in its scabbard, secured the folds of his cape so it would stay out of his way in the fight, and headed off, Lee to his right and slightly behind.

He lifted a hand as he drew close. "Evening, gentle sirs. Happen to know what they're serving for dinner tonight?"

One of the mercenaries stared. "You're that one. The Lindworm Slayer. Aren't you?"

"I suppose I am," Cimar said with a sigh. "I wish people were this excited about the indexing system I created for the archives. I'm much prouder of that than who or what I've killed. How do you know me, good sir?"

"Who doesn't know you if they've been in town more than ten minutes?" another mercenary muttered. "It's all they bloody talk about."

Cimar made a face. "I apologize, and I mean that sincerely. That sounds utterly tedious, and I have as much ego as any knight."

Beside him, Lee snorted.

One of the men looked at him, expression sharpening.

Cimar drew his sword and slammed the pommel into the man's nose, then kicked his feet out and turned on the man who'd first spoken, grabbing his head and slamming it into the wall behind him.

Nearby, out of immediate sight, he could hear Lee engaging more of the mercenaries.

Cimar managed to take out one more, this one regrettably fatal, before even more came surging out of the inn and, as he'd feared, still more from the stables. Though he hated to leave Lee to his own devices, no matter how well he could handle himself, they'd made a plan, and he wouldn't break from it because he wanted to fret like a parent.

Instead he slammed a gauntleted fist into the face of the young, stupid man that rushed him with little thought beyond 'charge.' The next couple were far more experienced, but still no match for Cimar. These bastards should try working in a library for a single day.

After he'd cut those two down, he moved on to the next. And the next.

There were screams and shouts around him, but all he focused on was the next sword, the sound of movement coming too hard and fast, the stench of blood filling his nostrils, the sweat sticking his hair to his face and stinging his eyes.

By the time the fighting ceased, he was

battered, bruised, and utterly exhausted. That was just one thing the ballads always left out: how fucking *exhausting* fighting was, even for the best trained knights.

He wiped sweat from his brow with a relatively clean bit of tunic and looked around for Lee—and stopped short as he took in the scene by the barn.

Ice. The puddle that had been there, left over from an early morning rainfall, was iced over, and it was clear more than one mercenary hadn't realized that until too late. He looked up, saw Lee standing nearby, slumped against a wall looking as wrung out as Cimar felt. "Since when can you do ice?"

"Since about a month ago. First time I've used it outside of practice, though." He shoved his sword into its sheath. "Damned useful."

Cimar just shook his head, too impressed to form words. Lee really was shaping up to be a mage-knight of legend. He'd leave Cimar in the dust one day, and Cimar couldn't wait to see it. "Come on, let's go find your lovers."

Lee rushed ahead of him into the inn, magic gleaming at his fingertips—but if there had been any mercenaries lingering inside, they'd opted for a strategic retreat. Cimar motioned he'd take care of sorting out any lingering problems that might be around, and Lee continued on through the dining room through a door in the back.

Sighing, sheathing his sword and drawing a knife instead, better to work with in the confined space, Cimar started at the top and worked his way down, ensuring no threats remained.

When that was done, he went back outside and secured two of the mercenaries for questioning. By the time Lee reappeared, he'd also secured a cart and had his horse brought, and Lee's from the stable.

The happy greeting died on his lips, though, as he took in Lee's tear-stained eyes and the anguish cutting deep lines into his young face. "Lee, what's wrong?"

Lee swallowed, hands curling and uncurling at his sides as he tried to calm himself. "It's what you thought: they took Everard and Odilia hostage, kept Odilia locked away in a storage room. Told Everard to reveal me when I showed up. Everard managed to convey a message to the bartender so I'd come to no harm. They'd intended to kill me to cripple you, make it look like a bar brawl gone wrong."

"Are they all right?"

"They're fine," Lee said, and looked ready to cry again. "Not willing to 'put up with this sort of thing' a second time, though."

Fury filled Cimar, but he tamped it down. Lee didn't need anger right now. He needed comfort. "I'm sorry, Lee. I know you cared deeply for them. It's unfortunate they proved unworthy of your affections."

Lee nodded but didn't speak.

Cimar wished he could do something, anything, to take his pain away. Only time could ease such wounds, though. "Head back with the cart; I'll follow shortly." When Lee frowned, Cimar added, "I want to pay for damages and such. I won't do or say anything untoward."

Though Lee clearly didn't believe him, he also looked like he wanted desperately to be as far away from the Gold Cock as possible. He nodded and all but ran for his horse.

Once Cimar was certain he had control of his temper, he strode into the inn and back into the dining room, where he predictably found those he sought. "Master Everard? Mistress Odilia?" He removed one of his gauntlets and set it on the table that stood between him and the couple.

They stiffened, staring fearfully, and Everard tentatively said, "Yes, Sir Knight?"

"It's Cimar, but I think you know that," Cimar replied. He reached into the purse in the pouch at the small of his back and withdrew three coins, slapping them on the table. "To cover damages to your home and business."

"I— Thank you, Sir Cimar. That is most gracious," Everard replied quietly, not looking at him.

Odilia tentatively met his gaze, but immediately dropped her eyes. "Is Lee all right?"

"Sir Leonine," Cimar snapped, causing

them both to look up. "The formal knighting won't take place until my challenge is concluded, but he was granted his spurs by Princess Korena just a few days ago. You'll address him properly, unless you've some reason to speak so informally of him."

Everard flinched. "Apologies, my lord. We did not mean to speak so rudely."

Cimar withdrew his hand and restored his gauntlet. "He risked a great deal for you today, you know. Not to belittle your efforts. What you did to save him—that was noble and brave of you, worthy of any ballad. So I don't understand why now you've spurned him. He risked quite literally everything for you. If we had been wrong in our suppositions, if the bartender had told the truth and we'd misjudged the situation... he would have lost those newly won spurs. He's been studying to be a knight since he was a child of ten. That's fourteen years—and he's won his spurs years earlier than most do. All of that, he risked to save you, and in return you spit in his face and leave him with a broken heart. But I promised him I'd not lash out at you, so this is where I stop. So far as I'm concerned, you've only proved you were never worthy of him. Good day, good sir, gentle lady."

He turned neatly on his heel and strode out, mounting his horse and riding off toward the castle, where his day was probably only about to get longer and uglier. He'd had enough of Tekker and Grayne's scheming and cheating. This was the last straw.

The challenge would end tonight, one way or another.

CHAPTER NINE

Davrin clapped along with everyone else as the jugglers finished their performance and signaled a servant for more wine as it faded off. Beside him, beautiful and imperious, Korena already looked more like a queen than a princess, while on her left His Majesty looked like a slovenly drunk who'd sat at the wrong table.

It only took skimming the room to see he was not the only one with that impression.

On His Majesty's other side, Tekker was speaking to him in low tones. Try as he might, Davrin could catch none of it. Neither could Korena, though it was clear she was doing all she could without tipping into drawing attention.

Whatever their latest scheme, Davrin would not let it succeed. A few more days and the final challenge would be called, and this whole affair would be behind them. Tekker and Grayne would be neutered of all their power; Ballior would be able to rest in peace; Davrin could focus on his pending marriage and his new relationship with Cimar.

Hopefully, he'd see Cimar later that

evening.

Thanking the servant for the wine, he sipped at it and then set the cup aside. "What do you think—" he stopped, along with everyone else in the crowded great hall, as the main doors were shoved open, letting in a blast of frigid air. Normally, the doors were kept closed, only a smaller one cut into one of the big ones used.

Davrin shot to his feet as Cimar strode into the room, dressed in full armor and so angry Davrin half-expected his armor to shoot sparks. Behind him came Leonine, dragging along two men bound heavily in chains, and behind them were more knights wearing the tunic of the royal guard.

"Cimar, are you all right? Sir Leonine?"

"We're fine," Cimar said, "though only because we're both vastly more skilled than the cheap thugs Tekker and Grayne hired to kill Sir Leonine."

King Rorlen stared coldly at Cimar. "That is a bold accusation, knight. For your sake, you'd better have a way to back it up."

"I do," Cimar said, and motioned to Leonine, who dragged forward the captured guards. "Speak."

The mercenary on the left remained silent, but the one on the right said, "Him, right there. The lord in the red tunic and the knight beside him. They hired us. Wanted the young one dead so as to rattle the knight, so he'd be unfit for combat come some stupid duel."

Rorlen looked unimpressed. "Why should I trust that Sir Cimar is not paying you to speak thus?"

At that, the second man stirred. "He's not. That man right there in the red tunic, Lord Tekker. He hired us. Exactly like my friend said. Nobles do it all the time. They want an edge in a fight or some discussion of some law or another, in a trade session… whatever. This one was no different. Wanted the young knight dead so the older one wouldn't fight as well. Paid us a hundred upfront, with another hundred to be paid when the job was done. I still have the money."

At his words, one of the guards who'd helped drag them in threw a purse to the ground. The clink of coins was unmistakable.

"Further statements can be collected from the innkeeper and his wife, the bartender, and still others," Cimar said. "This is flagrant cheating, and worse, it was attempted murder, and this challenge was called to bring justice for a murder in the first place."

Rorlen looked furious, and beside him Tekker finally had the decency to start looking worried. Behind him, standing against the wall, Grayne just looked annoyed at being bothered. "So what are you demanding, Sir Cimar? An end to the challenge? To call it off on grounds of cheating and tampering?"

"No," Cimar said. "I want the duel *now*. I

want this over and done with, once and for all. When it's over, I want those two banished for life."

"That is not your request to make," Rorlen snarled.

"It is when they cheat and try to kill my recently promoted squire!" Cimar bellowed, and Davrin would have sworn it sounded like his voice held an honest to gods *growl*.

Before Rorlen could order his head removed, which was clearly what he wanted to do for not just being disrespected, but in his own hall in front of his entire court, Tekker stood as well. "We answer the demand, with the caveat that for your dishonor, it will be a fight to the death."

Davrin barely kept from climbing on the table so he could get at the bastard to knock his teeth down his throat.

"Accepted," Cimar said, voice ringing out across the hall and effortlessly over all the racket, leaving a resounding silence in his wake.

Grayne smirked from where he remained at his post behind Tekker's seat, standing against the wall like the world's ugliest statue. "You really think you can best me, little librarian?"

"Come and find out."

"Not in the hall," Korena said with a sigh. "To the tournament field. The duel begins in one hour. Sir Cimar, I would speak with you privately."

Davrin offered his arm and escorted her from the hall, heart pounding in his throat all the while. They retreated to her private solar, where Aliara was already pouring drinks.

He'd just sat down with the glass Aliara handed him when the door opened. All but throwing the drink aside, Davrin rose and strode across the room to pull Cimar into his arms. "What in the world were you thinking, you knave?"

Cimar didn't reply immediately, just held tightly and rested his head against Davrin's chest. All his armor meant it wasn't a terribly comfortable arrangement, but Davrin didn't much give a damn.

"He's going to do everything in his power to kill you," Davrin said, the words coming out harsh, ragged. "Given he's a hellhound, there is a great deal within his power."

"I can handle him," Cimar said, drawing back and frowning up at him. "Do you really think I would have agreed to any of this if I didn't know, with absolute certainly, that I could handle Grayne? It was always going to come down to a fight. These things always do—and Grayne can't help but fight dirty, so my life was always on the line. Stop acting like you don't know that."

"You're right, you're right," Davrin said, and dragged him into a kiss, leaving his own lips stinging and bruised from the force of it. "That doesn't mean I have to like it. I never enjoyed that part of calling for a challenge. It's stupid that to have vengeance for my friend I must risk every life but my own."

Cimar smiled. "You're a terrible lord, actually caring about things like other people's lives. Entirely too soft to be a prince consort, surely."

Korena laughed, drawing their attention to where she stood closer to the fire with Aliara twined around her. "He is soft, but he's smart and pretty. Two out of three isn't bad."

Rolling his eyes, Davrin returned to his seat, liking it a bit too much when Cimar took up the traditional post of a champion: just to the right and slightly behind Davrin's chair. "What did you want to speak to Cimar about?"

"Nothing, really," Korena said. "I thought you two would like a moment. I have every faith Sir Cimar will take the day, but I also have every faith that Grayne will use every nasty, dirty trick in existence."

Cimar nodded. "Agreed."

"We'll give you two a moment. When you're done, we'll be waiting in the hall. Davrin, wear your ring. I want Tekker and everyone else to know just how badly they've messed up. If they want to play games, then let the games begin in earnest."

"My queen."

Korena swept out, Aliara at her side, the door closing quietly behind them.

"I will never be able to repay you for all you've done," Davrin replied. "I knew you would have to fight. You should not have to take a life.

That goes against everything we called this challenge for."

"When you treat with rats, death is inevitable."

Davrin kissed him, soft and slow and lingering, savoring the taste of this man he'd loved from afar for so long. "I've waited a lifetime to have you close. If you are parted from me now, I will lose my mind."

"Have faith in your champion," Cimar replied, and gave him a far more bitey kiss. "I've been waiting too, hoping in vain for what I thought would be eternity. I'm not going to let some rabid dog like Grayne take me away now."

"I have more faith in you than the divine. It's cheating rats I worry about. I will trust you to know how to handle the bastard."

"That reminds me..." Cimar stepped back far enough he could reach up and unbuckle the white collar that Davrin had never seen leave his neck, not even when they were in bed together. "Keep this for me?"

"Of course." Davrin wrapped the collar around his wrist like a band or brace, buckling it in place. "I'm sorry it's come to this too."

Cimar laughed. "It won't kill me. I don't like all the attention. But nothing could possibly draw more than being the lindworm slaying champion of the prince consort, so..." He shrugged one shoulder. "Now wish me luck, my prince, and let's put this matter to bed once and for all."

Davrin dragged him into one last, searing kiss, holding fast to either side of his head and devouring his mouth like it was the last meal he'd ever have. "You don't need luck," he said, voice ragged. "I do, however, promise that I will make all this strife, present and future, worthwhile every single day of our lives."

"I like that better." Reluctantly withdrawing, he pressed a closed fist to his chest, over his heart, in a traditional salute of fealty, then turned smartly on his heel and led the way from the room. Davrin removed the ring from around his neck as they walked, and by the time they stepped into the hall it was on his finger. Betrothed to the crown princess, future prince consort, for all the world to see now.

He offered his arm to Korena, who took it with a pleased smile. "You make a handsome pair, you and your champion." She waggled her eyebrows, a playful smirk curving her pretty mouth. "Maybe Aliara and I should test your mettles sometime."

"Honestly, Ren, I'm surprised it's taken you this long to make such a lecherous decision." Aliara cast Davrin a look that was equal parts fondness and exasperation. "Please ignore Her Highness's terrible attempts at soliciting a foursome. Orgy. Whatever it is at that point."

"I think for it to qualify as an orgy there must be at least five," Cimar said blandly, as though discussing a treatise on the average crop yield over the span of a decade. "Don't ask me how I know."

"Oh, I'm going to ask," Korena retorted.

Davrin and Aliara lifted their eyes to the ceiling.

Sadly, they then passed through the doorway that took them back to the public spaces of the castle, and then out into the great hall itself, beyond the walls of the castle, and to the fairgrounds.

The air was bitingly cold, the kind of cold that hurt to breathe in, left the lungs full of needles and the face frozen within moments. Even the fine furs they wore only did so much to keep them from being miserable.

Well, him and Korena and Aliara. If Cimar was affected by the cold, he gave no sign of it. He was as calm and collected and beautiful as on the morning he'd presented himself as Davrin's champion, angering King Rorlen and genuinely concerning Grayne and Tekker, despite their attempt at acting otherwise.

As they reached the private royal entrance of the fairgrounds, Leonine stepped clear of the crowds. He was carrying Cimar's shield on his back—not the usual buckler used in most duels, either, but a full-sized battle shield. He was holding the reins to their horses and lifted a hand in greeting. "Sir Cimar! Oh! Your Highness, my lady, your pardon." He knelt in the snow, smooth and graceful, and rose just as easily when Korena bid him do so. "Your lordship. May your noble champion take the day." His mouth twitched, and breaking formality he said, "Not that victory is hard when one is fighting a rabid dog with one trick to his name, and that trick quite old and used up."

"What have I told you about being cocky?" Cimar asked lightly, the reprimand ruined by a soft laugh.

Leonine grinned unrepentantly. "It's not cocky if it's true."

Cimar sighed. "Let's go, rapscallion. Your Highness, my lady, thank you for allowing me to walk with you. My lord, I will bring you victory."

"Just stay alive," Davrin said, hating he couldn't drag Cimar in for one last kiss. He watched as Cimar and Leonine walked away, and once they were out of sight escorted Korena and Aliana to the royal box.

King Rorlen was already there, Tekker alongside him like always. Normally the box was full of toadies and other guests, but right then there was only the five of them. Korena and Rorlen shared a look, some indecipherable conversation between king and crown princess, father and daughter.

Whatever was said, Rorlen wasn't happy about it, but he only grunted and motioned for all of them to sit.

Davrin bowed respectively and went

through the usual platitudes, then took his place at Korena's side. Strange that it was already becoming second nature to do so.

Servants came up with hot mulled wine, and Davrin took one gratefully. Still others stepped forward with lap blankets and hot stones. "Thank you." As the servants faded off, he turned to Korena. "I don't think I've ever seen this place so crowded."

"Everyone loves a good fight to the death," Korena said, voice level, but with underlying bitterness. "All the more exciting when it's against the Hellhound of Darmount and the new, exciting and popular Lindworm Slayer."

"At least they'll be too busy squabbling over their tasteless bets to get into much other trouble tonight."

Korena didn't roll her eyes, but the look she cast him conveyed it all the same. "You know people better than that."

Davrin laughed. "One can always hope."

The conversation lapsed as Rorlen lifted a hand and the trumpets obediently sounded. Standing, he hauled himself to the railing and bellowed out, "Today we conclude the challenge of Lord Davrin Dweller-by-the-Sea against Lord Tekker Malden. Champions, present yourselves."

Crossing the field, Grayne and Cimar knelt before the royal box, heads bowed low.

"At your personal request, this challenge had been declared a fight to the death. I declare this fight no holds barred. May the greatest win. To your corners."

Cimar rose smoothly to his feet, briefly caught Davrin's eyes, and offered the barest whisper of a smile, then strode off to the far right corner of the arena. There, still acting as his squire though he was technically no longer required to, Leonine slid his shield into place and fit his helmet onto his head. Finally, he handed Cimar his sword and slapped his chest as a sign of readiness and good luck.

In the opposite corner, two servants had been enlisted to awkwardly assist Grayne with his equipment, and it wasn't hard to tell nobody was happy with the arrangement. Grayne had had a squire once, but the poor boy had run off in the night after just two months. Davrin was amazed he'd lasted that long.

When both men had signaled they were ready, flags went up to notify the audience the start was eminent. A hush swept through the crowd, the tension lingered…lingered…

King Rorlen lifted a hand, the guards nearby struck the gong, and the fight was on.

Grayne surged for, all aggression and determination. He lacked finesse but more than made up for it with sheer brute force. Cimar was his opposite: slighter, relying on finesse and dexterity to supplement the strength that did not match Grayne's.

In skill, they were equally matched, well-trained knights with years of experience behind them, even if Cimar had spent most of his time in the archives.

Back and forth across the snow-ridden field they fought, exchanging bone-jarring blows that would leave them covered in bruises, knocking each other over, slamming occasionally into a wall. Davrin was exhausted watching after just a few minutes, the tension coiling in his stomach making him nauseous.

Grayne bellowed as he blocked a blow, feinted, and managed to kick Cimar's feet out from under him, sending him crashing to the ground, shield sliding away. Cimar blocked the blow that came slashing down at him, managing to catch the flat of the blade against his left vambrace. The blow must have left his arm throbbing, if not full out hurting, but he only rolled away as Grayne wasted precious seconds recovering from the stupidly flashy move and regained his feet. Then he darted away quickly, putting space between them. In place of the shield he could not safely retrieve, Cimar drew a long dagger secured at his back.

Laughing derisively, Grayne resumed his brutal assault, keeping the blows hard and fast, giving Cimar no chance to do anything except defend. As Cimar faltered from the force of one and stumbled back, Grayne lifted his sword and went in for another flashy finishing blow. Cimar ducked and rolled, regained his feet and sheathed his dagger in one smooth move, and scooped up some of the snow around them. As Grayne turned, Cimar threw it in his face, right over the open portion of his helmet, wider than was usual, and open all the way across to give Grayne better vision.

As Grayne snarled and cursed and tried to get the snow out of his eyes, Cimar moved in lightning fast, slamming a fist into his face right where he'd thrown the snow. That sent Grayne reeling, and from there it was easy enough to knock him off his feet.

Cimar straddled him and drew his dagger, slipping it in the gap between the gorget and breastplate, which shouldn't have been possible unless the armor wasn't put on exactly right, or if the aventail that went under it wasn't worn. Grayne had been lazy, or sloppy, or more likely had put on most of his armor alone and had paid the price.

Whatever was said between them, Davrin couldn't hear it from so great a distance, but Grayne lifted a hand in surrender. The crowds around them were a mix of congratulatory applause and resounding booing cries that Cimar hadn't killed him as ordered.

But a knight always had the prerogative to show mercy, even when ordered to fight to the death. Davrin simply hadn't expected the opportunity to present or for Grayne to accept it.

Cimar rose and offered a hand, but Grayne

knocked it away and said something that caused Cimar to shrug, sheath his dagger and sword, and turn away.

He hadn't gone more than a few steps when Grayne climbed to his feet, and even at a distance Davrin could see his eyes were glowing a terrible fiery red.

Davrin surged forward, gripping the railing of the royal box. "Cimar! Behind!"

Cimar didn't bother to turn around, just started running, putting as much space as he possibly could between him and Grayne. All the while, he discarded whatever bits and pieces of armor he could, including his sword belt.

Steam filled the arena as Grayne finished shifting. He stood at least nine measures tall, black fur a cut of shadow in the snow-drenched world around them, the tips like glowing embers. It was thick and heavy, sticking out in ragged spikes that looked more like weapons that fur. Snow turned to steam in a circle around him, and the ground hissed beneath his feet where it was scorched away. His nostrils billowed more steam, and the people nearest him in the arena seats grimaced and withdrew.

He roared, the sound echoing off the stone walls of the arena, making more than a few people recoil. Many simply got up and left, unwilling to stay for the death they'd cheered for now that it was going to be so grisly.

Across the field, close to the royal box,

Cimar stood calmly, at least half his armor discarded now.

Grayne snorted and huffed, head jerking in a way that seemed to taunt and goad.

"I gave you a chance to surrender," Cimar said, voice ringing out across the field. "I gave you a chance to live."

Grayne just snorted derisively again and tensed, feet digging deep into the muddy ground around him—then he was off, shooting across the field, headed straight for Cimar.

Who stood calmly. The air shimmered and wavered around him, like sunlight coming off hot stone, and then he was shifting, clothes and the remaining pieces of armor ripping and breaking apart as he grew in size.

And grew. And grew.

Grayne drew up just short of reaching him, and with a snort drew back out of the way, not stupid enough to get swept up in the uncontrollable thrashing of a large shifter.

Davrin wasn't the only one left reeling, gasping, as Cimar finished.

He was a dragon. An enormous, dark silvery-blue dragon with swirling silver eyes and four thick, sharp black horns. He dominated the arena and made Grayne look like a child—or a toy.

Seeming to realize his mistake at last, Grayne turned to flee, but it was far too late. A single burst of motion, a long, smooth lunge, and

Cimar had Grayne in his jaws. A hard crunch, and that was that. Cimar spit Grayne out then whipped around and bellowed at the royal box.

Tekker looked so ashen Davrin expected him to pass out.

King Rorlen, however, simply looked furious like usual. He surged to his feet, face red, body trembling with the force of his rage. "This is all your fault!" Before anyone could ask who exactly he was talking to, he punched Tekker in the face, sending him toppling to the ground. Surging forward again, Rorlen picked him up and dragged him into a position that Davrin recognized far too late.

"Father, no!" Korena screamed.

Too late. Rorlen snapped Tekker's neck and threw his body over the railing with far too much ease, then rounded on the rest of them. Nearby, the guards stood stupefied. Terrified.

Rage and madness filled Rorlen's eyes as he leveled them on Davrin. "It's all your fault, and you're going to pay. Right now. I won't tolerate this a second longer."

"Father, stop it! Just stop it!"

The words were of no avail, however, as Rorlen lunged at them, even as Cimar roared and Korena yelled for the guards to do their job.

In the small confines of the royal box, there was nowhere to go. Davrin could only brace himself and hope he lived.

CHAPTER TEN

Brilliant light burst in the royal box even as Cimar roared and lunged that way. It was bright enough he had to close his inner eyelids, which stripped much color from the world and made things somewhat blurry.

He could still see well enough though to realize he knew that light. That magic. He'd just never seen it at that scale before. Leonine.

Sure enough, as the light faded and Cimar could open his inner eyelids to see properly again, there was Lee, standing in front of Davrin with sword drawn and his left hand thrown out, sparks still dancing around his fingers in the aftermath of the spell.

King Rorlen, momentarily stupefied, returned to his murderous mission with a bellow of rage.

But Lee had gained Cimar all the time he needed to close the remaining distance, grab King Rorlen in his jaws, and spit him out onto the arena floor. He growled as Rorlen slowly climbed to his feet, stumbling about like a drunk. His eyes were filled with mad rage when he finally looked up.

"You're nothing!" Rorlen raged. "Nothing at all! You're a knight and your duty is to obey me! Stand down at once! You'll have your head removed for—" Rorlen broke off as blood flew from his lips right as a barrage of arrows pierced his chest.

Cimar roared and recoiled, summoning his magic to shift back to his human form. He dropped with a groan to the ground as it finished, and only barely heard people calling his name.

Barely a breath later, there were people everywhere in the arena: guards, officials, Princess Korena trying to regain order.

Cimar ignored it all, unable to focus on more than himself right then, exhausted and wrung out. He hadn't wanted the fight to go the way it had, but he wasn't surprised either. The stupid questions and comments hadn't even started yet, and he was already sick of them.

"Cimar!" Davrin dropped down beside him and immediately dropped his own cloak around Cimar's shoulders. "Are you all right?"

"Just tired."

"Lee is coming with your belongings. Come on, let's get out of the middle of all this. I do not envy whoever just sent a volley of arrows into His Majesty. The kingdom might thank him, but the law has other opinions."

Cimar laughed faintly. "Have fun helping your wife sort that mess out, Your Highness."

Davrin groaned. "Now is not the time to be

mocking me for that, you knave. Oh, here's Lee."

"Sir Cimar!" Lee dropped a large satchel and set of saddlebags on the ground in front of them. "Are you all right? Any injuries?"

"Nothing of note. I think shifting took care of it all," Cimar replied. "Come on, let's get me on my feet and away from this mess, so I can get dressed without waving my cock at the entire royal guard and half the city."

"More like three fourths of the city," Davrin said, and waved off Lee before helping Cimar himself. "I think they're all still distracted by the abrupt murder of our king, so you and your dick are safe for now."

"Now who's the knave?" Cimar grumbled, yawning before he'd barely finished the words as they headed away from the arena and through a door to the chambers used by combatants for training, cleaning, and so forth.

They came to a halt in one of the changing rooms, and Cimar handed back Davrin's cloak as Lee opened the satchel and pulled out Cimar's clothes. In short order, he was in warm, dry clothes free of tears and bloodstains. Lee next pulled out armor—lightweight leather stuff, but all he should need for whatever came next, as his two biggest problems were now dead. Thank the gods for their mercy that nobody could ever accuse him of having killed the king. Grabbing him and throwing him around, yes, but he'd been very much alive and well before that arrow volley.

"Managed to retrieve this too," Lee said, and only then did Cimar notice he'd slung Cimar's sword belt over one shoulder. He held it out, and Cimar couldn't deny he felt infinitely better as he strapped it into place.

Cimar hugged him. "I'm going to be lost without you, but I will be happy to finally have you officially as my peer, Lee."

"Wouldn't be here without you," Lee said gruffly, and hugged him again before letting go. "Shall we return to the fracas?"

Davrin sighed. "I'd much rather not, but my fiancée would probably like my assistance. Let's go then, noble champion and victor of the challenge."

Cimar echoed his sigh, because a victory had seldom felt so hollow. There was satisfaction in knowing Ballior had been avenged and could rest in peace. In knowing the guilty parties had paid for their crimes. He would have preferred they faced proper justice, however. That he wasn't stuck with the taste of Grayne's blood in his mouth and the knowledge of how it felt to crunch him, kill him. The stupid bastard should have held to his surrender.

Shoving the gloomy thoughts aside, he drew his sword and motioned to Davrin. "Stay behind me. Lee, take up the rear. Whoever fired those arrows could be more than willing to fire some more."

Davrin nodded, Lee fell into position, and

they quickly rejoined the chaos in the arena.

It had been quelled, somewhat, the people having been removed or at least driven to the edges and out of the way. Guards were standing watch, an entire circle around King Rorlen's body. Korena stood in the center of the chaos, Aliana to her left, speaking with Joffrey, Captain of the Guard, and several others. She turned her head slightly as they approached, and Cimar didn't think he imagined the relief that showed ever so briefly in her eyes as they landed on Davrin. He knew the feeling well.

Motioning to the guards keeping anyone from getting close to her, voice pitched to be heard, she said, "Let my fiancé and his knights through." As Davrin approached, she extended a hand and pulled him close, looping their arms together.

Cimar took up position to Davrin's right, and Lee stood close by, both their swords still drawn.

"Do we know who?" Davrin asked, as Joffrey bowed and departed, walking with impressive deftness across the snow and ice.

Korena shook her head. "No. Soldiers have been sent out to the likeliest positions of the shooter, but by the time we reach it they'll be long gone. Right now we're simply waiting for the crowds to clear enough we can safely escort his body back to the castle."

"You shouldn't be out in the open like this."

"I feel if they wanted me dead alongside my father, they'd have already done it," Korena said. "Be that as it may, you're not wrong. I am going to escort my father's body personally, though, no matter what the risk." She looked briefly sad but mostly just tired. "He was..." she sighed and fell silent.

Davrin smiled softly and covered her hand with his free one. "I understand."

"Thank you."

Cimar didn't smile watching them, but only because it would ill suit his current post.

Mercifully, a few minutes later Captain Joffrey returned, bowing quickly before saying, "Your Majesty, we're ready to move out. I've a cart waiting for His Majesty, and a full escort for him. The roadway has been secured clear to the gates. Your horses are being brought."

"Thank you, Captain," Korena replied, even as a pair of knights came up leading the horses. A couple more came behind them a moment later bearing Cimar and Lee's horses.

When the whole party was mounted up, and the king's body had been carefully loaded onto the cart, draped in borrowed cloaks and flowers that had been intended for the challenge victor, Korena gave the signal and the process moved out.

It was a somber affair, more somber than Cimar would have expected, given how universally Rorlen had been hated, secretly and sometimes not so secretly. The murder of a king was still the murder of a king, though. The icy wind and falling snow didn't help anything.

By the time they reached the castle, dark was falling, and he couldn't feel any part of his body, it was all so thoroughly frozen.

As they finally reached the great hall, Korena paused to speak with Captain Joffrey once more. "Secure the body in his private courtyard and have the pyre ready for after morning prayers. That should be enough time to arrange everything properly."

"Yes, Your Majesty," Joffrey replied.

The body would freeze, being out in the cold all night, and Cimar was eternally grateful to the divine that was not his problem to solve.

Joffrey strode off, likely to inflict the unenviable task on whoever he found first, and Korena waved off everyone else seeking her attention, relegating the task of dealing with them to the nearby Steward Lander, who was probably greatly concerned she might shortly be out of job with the king dead and a queen of very different mind on the throne.

Korena headed off, still escorted by Davrin with Aliana at her side. Cimar took over the lead, with Lee taking up the rear again, until they reached Korena's private chambers, at which point he took up position on the wall opposite, facing the knights guarding the door. Korena, Davrin, and Aliana vanished inside, and Cimar sighed as the door closed. Safe, or as safe as they could get, for a little while.

"What a day," Lee said. "I didn't think it could get worse than being summarily tossed out by my lovers, but I vastly underestimated the universe. I am sorry, Cimar, it feels like in all of this your victory has been completely lost."

Cimar snorted. "My victory is the least important matter today. Ballior has his vengeance, that is all I ever cared about."

"Yeah, you didn't do this just so you could make eyes at Lord Dweller-by-the-Sea at all."

"Shut it, rapscallion," Cimar said, even as the nearby guards struggled not to crack their somber miens. "Now isn't the time for such jests."

Lee's mouth twitched briefly. "I dunno, a bit of levity seems good right now, and there's never a bad time to tease you, Sir Cimar."

"Hahaha," Cimar said, and that time the guards did briefly crack.

They stood there nearly an hour, to judge by the light and the distant tolling of the temple bell, but it could have been more or less. Cimar was long ready for sleep by the time the door opened. To his surprise, though, Davrin beckoned them to come inside rather than stepping out.

Frowning, Cimar obeyed, Lee close behind. Davrin closed the door quietly behind them and led the way to a large sitting room. Korena rose from where she'd been sitting with Aliana, a beautiful, imposing, but still approachable queen, nothing remotely like her terrifying father.

"Sir Cimar, I am sorry that in this abrupt turn of events, your noble deeds have fallen by the wayside. You are victor of the challenge, and won that victory fairly and honorably, more than can be said of your fallen opponent. Formalities must wait, I'm afraid, but you are forthwith granted the Order of the Sovereign Rose."

"Yo— Your Majesty—" Cimar didn't know what to say. That merit had not been awarded for almost fifty years. It was one of the most difficult merits to achieve, and most of them wound up being awarded posthumously. He was only the eleventh to receive it while still alive. "I am humbled. Thank you, Your Majesty."

She smiled briefly. "As you are victor, and my fiancé's champion, I also offer you the position of royal champion, should you like to take up that mantle. You need not reply now, for the duty is not a light one. We'll speak again in a few days."

"Yes, Your Majesty."

Dismissing him, Korena turned her attention to Leonine. "Step forward, young sir, and kneel."

Lee's eyes widened, but he immediately obeyed.

Accepting the sword that Cimar offered her, Korena rested the flat of the blade briefly against the back of Lee's bowed head. "Do you swear to heed the vows of your knighthood and the commands of your queen and country?"

"I do so swear."

"Rise, then, Sir Leonine of Darting."

Leonine jerked his head up at that. "Of *Darting*."

She laughed and returned Cimar's sword. "Well, what is Grayne going to do with all that property? By rights it should go to Cimar, but I sensed he'd rather it go to you."

"Yes," Cimar said.

"Then so shall it be. Now the fun parts are concluded I must, alas, move on to business. Rise, Sir Leonine." When he'd stood, she continued, "I am afraid I must put you straight to work. Right now, with everything in upheaval, there are precious few persons I trust. I am appointing you to find my father's killer or killers and either bring me them, their heads, or a damned good explanation. Do you understand?"

"I understand, Your Majesty, and am honored to undertake such a task."

"Good. You can leave in the morning. There's little enough trail to follow anyway, so nothing to be accomplished by leaving immediately. I'm sure you'd like to be rested up too, especially after that impressive display back in the arena. You seem a mage of no small acumen."

"I have skill," Leonine said quietly. "Whether or not that's entirely a good thing, I've yet to decide. But it's saved lives, so I cannot complain."

"It's a burden as much as a blessing, as many such things are," Aliana said quietly from where she was still sitting close to the fire wrapped in blankets. "You show yourself well, young knight. Have faith in yourself, and I promise that people worthy of you will someday cross your path. Do not let the weak of heart weaken yours." She removed a hand from the blanket and cupped it with fingers spread, and little sparkles danced in her palm briefly before she withdrew the hand again.

"So you're the one who spelled my ring," Davrin said. "I had a guess."

"Thank you, my lady," Leonine said quietly, looking for a moment like he was going to cry. "If you will permit me, Your Majesty, I'd like to be off to prepare for my journey."

"Of course."

"We'll depart as well," Davrin said, "and leave you ladies in peace. I will see you in the morning." He took Korena's offered hand and kissed the back of it, then did the same to Aliana. Cimar and Leonine bowed, and the three of them departed.

Out in the hall, Cimar hugged Leonine tightly. "Have a care, Lee. Come home, I do not want to have seen you knighted only to immediately lose you."

"Going to take more than a few assassins to get me," Leonine said. "Now go away, I have things to do."

"See me before you leave," Cimar said, and gave him a playful push away before turning and heading in the opposite direction at Davrin's side. When they reached the main hallways, Cimar paused only to have one servant fetch some clothes and items from his own rooms to have brought to Davrin's, and another he sent to Croy in the armory. After that, they were entirely done with speaking to other people, or doing more than nodding as they kept walking,

It seemed to take years to reach Davrin's rooms, rooms that would not be his for much longer, given that it would only be weeks, if not days, before he was married and moved to the royal wing of the castle. Normally such a wedding would not take place until the mourning period was over, but given the grim circumstances…

"This has been a long, strange day," Davrin said as they finally reached his room, unlocking the door and pushing it open, and closing it firmly behind them before locking it again. He set the key on a nearby table and leaned against the door. "The kind of day you need a month of sleep to get over, but I'll be lucky to get a few hours before I must rise to help Korena with all that must happen before the burning ceremony."

"I have to see if I have clothes suitable for all we'll be doing the next several days," Cimar said with a laugh. "I'm not used to being so front and center, and I'm short a squire now to help me. I suppose I'll have to look into getting a new one."

"You're not going to have time for a squire, even if you don't want to be royal champion." Davrin immediately flinched and dropped his gaze. "I'm sorry, I'm making a lot of assumptions. You probably would love to go back to your quiet archives."

Cimar finished removing all his myriad layers, until he was only in hose and undertunic, then stepped into Davrin's space and twined arms around his neck. "I'm exactly where I want to be." He kissed Davrin softly and then drew back to add, "Anyway, now everyone is going to want to pester the mighty dragon that slew a lindworm and a hellhound and tossed around the king. My only hope for sanity is by being too busy and imperious while serving you for anyone to be allowed to approach me."

Davrin laughed and dragged him back in for a longer, vastly more thorough kiss. "You were magnificent," he said as they drew apart again. "A dragon. The chance of that is one in the thousands. No wonder you preferred to keep it to yourself. I've never seen a dark blue one, either. I thought dragons were always paler greens and browns and such."

"I have no idea," Cimar replied. "I've searched the archives high and low, and the only other blue dragon I can find mention of was in a kingdom nowhere close to ours. If there is rhyme or reason to the coloring, no one has figured it out yet. I'm also apparently larger than most dragons, though that's hard to say for certain. Suffice to say I am strange, and that is just one of the reasons I preferred to keep the matter private. Don't go apologizing yet again. I'd rather you just kiss me again before I fall asleep."

Smiling, Davrin gave the requested kiss, slow and sweet, as though savoring a rare treat. Cimar shivered and nuzzled him when they drew apart.

"I am happy you are mine at last, though I wish Ballior was here to tease us both over it."

"I'm sure he'll find a way, in this life or another," Cimar replied. "Now let's go to bed before I fall asleep on my feet."

"My knight," Davrin murmured as he playfully bowed Cimar toward the bed before setting to work on his own clothes.

When he reached the bed, Cimar stripped off his remaining clothes and hastily climbed beneath the covers.

Davrin threw more wood on the fire, then joined him, and Cimar immediately moved to cuddle close, so he could fall asleep his new favorite way: head on Davrin's chest, listening to his heartbeat.

~~*

The weather had grown worse overnight, and Cimar could not wait to go back to bed. He was far more worried about Leonine than himself, though. "I wish you'd wait until the weather calmed."

"I'd be waiting until spring," Leonine said with a laugh. "I'll be fine. It's not like I'm new to the miseries of winter weather."

"Have a care all the same."

Leonine smiled affectionately and tolerantly as he finished loading up his horse. "Is that why you insisted on seeing me off? To lecture me on being careful in the snow."

"No, you knave, I have gifts for you, but if you want to be flippant about my caring…"

"You know I'm not truly." Leonine finished with his saddlebags and turned fully to face him. "What have you, then, Sir Cimar? A token for my journey?"

"If I know you, you'll get plenty of tokens along the way," Cimar drawled. "No, my gifts are a bit more practical." He went over to the stacks of hay waiting to be dispensed amongst the horses and returned with two cases. One very obviously contained a sword. The other was smaller, square, and had arrived with the sword, though not on Cimar's command, but Korena's.

"Made from the lindworm skin," Cimar said as he handed over the long box.

Leonine set it on the ground and threw it open, and made a rough, incoherent noise as he took in the contents. Inside was a beautiful longsword, impressive even by Croy's near-impossible standards. The hilt was long enough to be gripped with one or two hands, and it could also be gripped by the blade itself, right at the base, to really punch through the weak points in plate. Set in the hilt was a jewel that seemed to never settle on a color, looking purple one moment and shifting to orange the next, like the sky of a rising or setting sun. The pommel had been carved into the likeness of a perching hawk, its eyes jewels to match the one in the pommel. "I've never seen such a fine sword."

"Well, Croy is the best in at least three kingdoms, and he had lindworm skin to work with. The jewels and hawk were his choices, but they seem fitting."

"Thank you, Sir Cimar." Leonine rose and removed his current sword, affixing it to his horse as a spare before buckling the new sword, and its matching dagger, into place.

Cimar smiled. "You can leave off the honorific now, you know. We're peers, equals. You're not my squire anymore."

Leonine returned the smile, happy and eager and a touch shy, as though he could not entirely believe he was awake. "It's a marvelous gift, Cimar. I cannot thank you enough."

"One more, though this is from Her Majesty," Cimar replied, and opened the box before turning it around to display the contents, which were exactly what he'd anticipated: spurs, shiny and new, also made from lindworm, with a jewel set in each that matched his sword and dagger.

"Those are my spurs? I didn't expect to… not until I returned."

"You are a knight, and should be properly fitted, even if we must skip most of the pomp and circumstance. Now hold still."

"No, you don't—" Leonine fell silent, clearly discomfited, as Cimar knelt and affixed the spurs. "You didn't have to do that."

Cimar gave him a look. "I was your mentor, and you have been one of my closest friends for many years. No one else was ever going to affix your first spurs. Now stop being a silly knave and get to work."

Leonine laughed, hugged him tightly, and took hold of the reins of his horse. "Fare thee well, Cimar. Hold the line while I'm gone."

"Far thee well, Leonine. Return to us hale and victorious."

Cimar watched him depart into the swirling white beyond the castle curtain, proud and happy and sad all at once. Then he turned and returned the keep, where his new life awaited him: a fine queen, her secret mage advisor, and a regal prince consort. All that lacked was a royal champion to keep them safe, and it took only a few more paces to reach them and assume that role for as long as he lived.

Fin

About the Author

Megan is a long-time resident of queer romance, and keeps herself busy reading and writing it. She is often accused of fluff and nonsense. When she's not involved in writing, she likes to cook, harass her wife and cats, or watch movies. She loves to hear from readers, and can be found all over the internet.

meganderr.com
patreon.com/meganderr
pillowfort.io/maderr
meganderr.blogspot.com
facebook.com/meganaprilderr
meganaderr@gmail.com
@meganaderr